MOROCCAN MYSTERY

Other Avon Camelot Books by
Thomas McKean

VAMPIRE VACATION

Coming Soon

THE ANTI-PEGGY PLOT

Born in New York, THOMAS MCKEAN has lived and worked in various parts of the United States, Europe, and North Africa. Among his various occupations, he has been a waiter, teacher, artist, storyteller, and writer and director of children's theatre. He resides in New York City.

MOROCCAN MYSTERY

Written and illustrated by

Thomas McKean

AN AVON CAMELOT BOOK

MOROCCAN MYSTERY is an original publication of Avon Books.
This work has never before appeared in book form.

AVON BOOKS
A division of
The Hearst Corporation
1790 Broadway
New York, New York 10019

Library of Congress Cataloging in Publication Data:

McKean, Thomas.
    Moroccan mystery.

    (An Avon Camelot book)
    Summary: Three children visiting Morocco become involved in dangerous adventures with a ring of kidnappers.
    [1. Kidnapping—Fiction. 2. Morocco—Fiction.
3. Brothers and sisters—Fiction] I. Title.
PZ7.M478658Mi 1986   [Fic]   85-26761

First Camelot Printing, June 1986

for:

Georges, Béatrice, Justine, &
Gaspard Formentelli
Hajiba Khaldouni
Jérôme Thélot
Denis & Anne-Marie Thélot-Penon

Contents

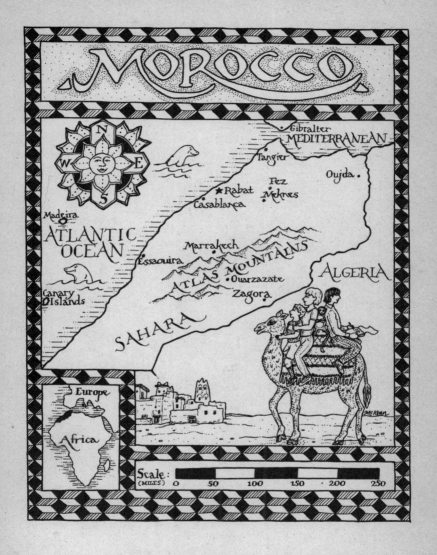

Chapter I

Taxis in Marrakech Are Beige and Black

They kidnapped Teasdale on our second day in Morocco.

He had gone out for a walk by himself just before lunch and when he hadn't returned by two o'clock we started to get nervous. By four o'clock, when there was still no sign of him, we all started going crazy with worry for our vanished brother.

"Christopher Columbus!" said Beth. "Where could he have gone?"

"The martians have him!" Leo replied. Leo, who's nine, is a firm believer in UFOs.

"Now, now," said our dad, "I'm sure he's just fine."

Finally, at six o'clock there was a sharp knock on the door that Beth raced to answer.

There was no one at the door—just the long slanting shadows and the silence of the empty street.

Beth was about to close the door when she noticed a small slip of paper crammed into a crack on the wall across the way. Ten seconds later found Beth pale and shaken, delivering the paper to our dad.

He read in stunned silence and then said, "Oh, my God!" in a strange voice. For there, on the paper, written in Teasdale's distinctive script, were the following words:

1

Oh dear Father, kidnapped I be;
Do what they ask if you want again to see me!
It's not very nice, but please don't you worry—
Do what they ask and I'll be home in a hurry!

P.S. They made me write this!

Below that there was the following message from the kidnappers, glued on the paper with torn-out letters from magazines:

Finally, at the bottom of the page, was Teasdale's signature:

Teasdale M. Smith

2

"We should never have come to Marrakech!" announced our Granny Bea in a trembling voice. "I must have been mad to permit such an expedition!"

In fact, our granny *had* been against the trip from the start.

"I don't care why you have to go," she'd told our dad, "I am quite convinced it is no place for children! Go alone and leave them with me!"

"No, Mother," our dad had replied. "We'll all go—you too! It'll be a family trip—my work in Marrakech shouldn't be too time-consuming."

"It's against my better judgement. . . ." responded our granny. But before two weeks had passed we'd arrived at the airport in Marrakech.

Our granny was not pleased to be in Morocco.

"Really!" she sniffed. "Just look at this airport! I am surprised we've arrived with our lives! The sooner you conclude your business here in Marrakech the better!"

"Now, Mother," said our dad; "it's not as bad as all that. According to my guidebook—"

"Fiddlesticks on your guidebook!" snorted our granny. "It is nothing but a pack of lies! Now where are our bags?"

We three kids ran off to look for our luggage, leaving our dad and Granny to discuss Morocco by themselves. We'd already decided we liked the country—even though all we'd seen was the airport. Here I have to add that it's one of the kids who's telling this story—though you'll have to guess which.

When we'd located our bags, we dragged them to our dad and Granny.

"Thank you, Beth," said our dad as Beth handed him his enormous suitcase. "This bag weighs a ton—I bet it was one big handful!"

"Oh, not for an athlete like me," replied Beth.

3

Leo meanwhile had appeared with one of Granny Bea's bags.

Finally Teasdale joined us. At ten, he's the middle kid in the family and he's a poet. Most of the time he even *talks* in poetry! He was carrying his multicolored velvet traveling case that contained more poetry books than it did clothes. Teasdale brushed his dark bangs off his pale forehead and said:

> "On Moroccan soil we stand,
> Below the blazing desert sun;
> As we explore this ancient land
> I hope that we have lots of fun!"

"So do I!" agreed Beth, and off we dashed to look for a taxi.

There were tons of taxis waiting outside—funny little beige cars with black roofs, called *"petit taxi,"* the word *"petit"* meaning small in French. Morocco was once a French colony so a good number of the people speak French, although the national language is Arabic. Some Moroccans speak a language called Berber; very few speak English. Luckily Granny Bea is fluent in French, and Teasdale and our dad can speak it pretty well. All Beth and Leo know are words like *"bonjour"* and *"merci beaucoup"* and things like that.

At least ten different taxidrivers descended on us for the honor of driving us to our destination. Granny Bea examined them painstakingly and selected the one she considered the cleanest.

"Cleanliness is the best policy!" she informed the taxidriver as he struggled to fit all our bags in the trunk of his small car.

"Oui, oui, madam," he smiled and kept on stuffing bags.

"See, Mother," said our dad, "the people here are very friendly."

"A bit too friendly, in my opinion," our granny replied. "Just look at that!" she added, pointing with one of her incredibly wrinkled but still strong fingers.

We followed the direction of her finger and saw a young girl who looked about Beth's age being pushed into a bright yellow Citroën by two robed Moroccans. She was saying, *"Mais non! Mais non!"* and didn't look very happy. This was taking place across the airport parking lot so we couldn't see too clearly what was going on.

"It is my belief," stated our granny, "that a person should be allowed free choice when it comes to which taxi he or she wishes to ride in!"

"But that isn't a taxi!" Leo pointed out.

"Of course it is!" replied our granny in a loud voice. "It's yellow, is it not?"

"Yeah," said Leo, "it's yellow—but taxis in Marrakech are always painted beige and black!"

"Oh," said Granny Bea quietly, not liking very much to be wrong.

At this moment our attention was called away by the taxidriver telling us he was ready to drive us into town.

As we piled in, our dad explained to the driver in his broken French that we were going to the home of Edward Greyley, located on Derb el Hammam.

Our driver told us Derb el Hammam was in the Mouassine section of town and not far from something called the Djemaa el Fna and we'd be there in less than twenty minutes. Granny Bea told him to keep his eye on the road and off we went.

Palm trees and small pink houses whizzed by us as we left the airport behind and approached Marrakech.

Our dad told us that Marrakech was a good-sized city, located in roughly the center of the country, and built over an oasis. He also told us that Marrakech was divided into two sections—a modern one called the New City or Guéliz, and an older one called the Old City, or Medina. He said we were bound for a home in the Medina.

"I just hope," he said, "that we were wise to agree to stay at Ed Greyley's, instead of a hotel. I doubt he's used to families—after all, he *is* a bachelor."

"Considering we've flown halfway around the world so you can help him with his business transactions, I would say it was the least he could do!" snapped Granny Bea. "And besides, I am quite sure I would not be able to sleep a wink in some fleabag hotel with a camel lodging in the next room no doubt, and who knows what other horrors!"

"Now, Mother," began our dad in his lawyer voice, "you know—"

"I know nothing of the kind!" retorted Granny Bea and told the driver to slow down.

We kids didn't care where we stayed. We were just plain excited to be in such a mysterious and strange place as Marrakech.

And, as Teasdale pointed out:

"A camel in the room next to me
Is something I would like to see!"

Chapter II

A Swan-Head Umbrella Comes in Handy

"Djemaa el Fna," said the taxidriver, stopping the car.

Our dad gasped and even Granny Bea didn't know what to say. Around us stretched an enormous square with over a thousand different things going on at one time. We could hear drumbeats and strange music and even from the taxi window we could see trained monkeys, acrobats, fortune-tellers, even a snake charmer.

"Christopher Columbus!" exclaimed Beth. "What is this place?"

Our dad, who'd been leafing through his guidebook, explained that we were in the Djemaa el Fna which is the central square in the old part of Marrakech.

The driver then told us that Mr. Greyley's house was on a road too small to drive on so we'd have to walk. Of course, he added, for a little bit extra he'd come along and show us the way.

Lugging our suitcases, we followed the driver across the Djemaa el Fna toward Derb el Hammam. The huge square was boarded with low pink buildings and on the horizon we could see a number of tall elegant buildings which Granny Bea told us were mosques, Muslim places of worship. They looked interesting, but not half as interesting as what we saw around us as we walked.

The Djemaa el Fna, Marrakech

The Djemaa el Fna was as big as a few football fields and jammed with thousands of people. Many were wearing the traditional Moroccan clothing of long robes, yellow slippers, and small hats or turbans. A number of the women had veils over their faces and streaks of makeup on their foreheads. We also saw a lot of hungry-looking children.

Passing a few vegetable markets, we walked by a more open area where lots was happening—we saw little old ladies in veils selling flat loaves of freshly-baked bread; and men, who must have been dentists, seated on dirty mats with rows of bloody teeth laid out in front of them.

We were so busy looking around us we didn't look to see exactly where we were going—and before we knew it, Teasdale had bumped into a wiry little man with hardly any teeth, narrow slits for eyes, and amazingly long fingernails. He was playing on a long silver instrument, a bit like a recorder. Too late we noticed the basket at his feet had started to wiggle. Then, coil by coil, an evil-looking cobra rose, swaying in the hot morning sun, its thin tongue darting in and out almost too fast to see. Suddenly the snake lunged at Teasdale—who promptly fainted.

He was immediately surrounded by at least fifty concerned Moroccans, some of whom tried pouring some dark liquid into his mouth. We all rushed to his side while Granny Bea cleared the crowd away with her swan-head umbrella. She then gave a brief speech in French informing the crowd that nothing was seriously wrong with Teasdale—he always faints when he gets frightened or upset.

Before long Teasdale revived and we continued on our way, though not before Granny Bea told the snake charmer what she thought of a grown man frightening a young boy with a cobra. But the snake charmer just grinned at her, baring three or four yellow teeth stained with something dark. Then he spat in our direction as Granny Bea hurried away from him.

Moments later we left the Djemaa el Fna and entered a narrow street about ten feet wide, crowded with people and bordered with small shops. It was shaded from the powerful Moroccan sun by woven-reed mats hung horizontally overhead. They cast wonderful striped shadows and somehow the total effect was like being under water.

We walked for about ten minutes on this street, passing shops full of all kinds of nuts and dried fruits, carts piled high with oranges, little cobbler stands, shops dark with old Islamic leather-covered books and shops bright with metal teakettles and brass trays. We strolled by a butcher's shop which had real cows' heads lying in an old cardboard box, but luckily Teasdale had his eye on a little donkey walking in front of us, pulling a load of sweet-smelling dried herbs Moroccans call *louisa,* so he didn't see them. If he had, I bet he would have fainted again.

"Tournez à droite," our taxidriver directed us. So we did—turn to the right, that is, under an archway and into the thinnest street you ever saw. It wasn't more than four feet wide and wound its way among tall pink and ochre walls—walls of all different heights, crumbling with age, with stucco, brick, and plaster falling all over. Sometimes the road would widen into triangular-shaped courts and then suddenly be narrow again. It reminded Beth of a maze. And along the way were small wooden doors, just Leo's size, brightly painted and held together with huge round spikes.

We turned left and then right, past alleyways and dead ends, then onto a straight short dead-end street. A cat miaowed on the dusty ground and from far above us we heard the prayers being wailed from the top of a mosque.

"Derb el Hammam," said the taxidriver.

11

"It means 'street of the bath'," explained our dad.

"Bath, did you say?" inquired Granny. "That sounds promising!"

It was no trouble finding Ed Greyley's house on the little street, so our dad gave the driver a few dirhams and knocked on a small green door.

We were all wondering what sort of house could be behind such a tiny door on such a tiny street when the door opened wide and a head with short brown hair and a big wide smile appeared.

"Well, I'll be!" it said. "James Smith and family, all safe and sound! Welcome to Marrakech! C'mon in!"

The voice belonged to Ed Greyley, an acquaintance of our dad who ran a computer company in Morocco. He'd moved to Marrakech about four months before to start his business and had just become partners with an Englishman named Lord Hodgson. A British banker named Nicholas Andrews had lent the company some money and was coming to Marrakech soon to look over the books before underwriting another loan to help them expand. That was why our dad was in Marrakech—to handle the legal documents for the new loan.

Ed Greyley was in his mid-thirties and was very big all over, like a football player.

We made our introductions in a low, dark hallway and then followed Ed into an immense and beautiful courtyard that formed the center of the house. It was covered with exquisite tiles, all brightly colored. In the middle was a fountain spurting water, and on either side of it were two orange trees at least forty feet tall and covered with oranges. The whole courtyard was big enough for a decent game of baseball. Overlooking it on two sides were a lot of windows and doors, also two large balconies.

12

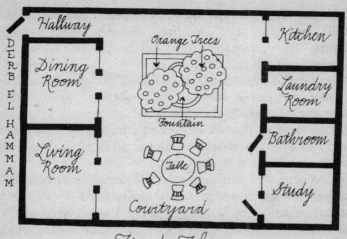

First Floor

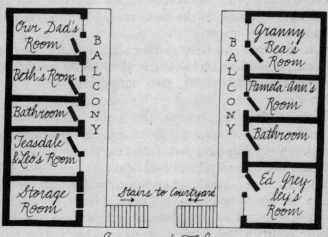

Second Floor

ED GREYLEY'S HOUSE

"Christopher Columbus!" exclaimed Beth. "What a house!"

"Yeah!" Leo agreed. "It would be perfect for a secret UFO landing!"

"It sure is something else," Ed added with a grin. "As they say here in old Marrakech, houses are built closed to the street but open to the sky."

Ed then showed us to our rooms, located on the far side of the courtyard, and told us tea would be served in twenty minutes, after we'd freshened up.

Our rooms were on the second floor, all overlooking the courtyard. Each room had beautifully tiled floors, carved wooden ceilings, thick white walls and small windows with green shutters. Above each door was an additional window to aid in ventilation. You got to the rooms by walking along the balcony and going in the right door—each room had its own door opening out onto the balcony. (Here Teasdale has added a diagram of the house, so you can see exactly what I'm talking about.)

Beth, our dad, and Granny Bea all got their own rooms, but Teasdale and Leo had to share. Besides our rooms, there were two other bedrooms, two bathrooms, and a locked storage room.

While we were unpacking, the most delicious scent of fresh peppermint wafted up from the courtyard. Our dad strolled in and explained that in Morocco they drink regular tea mixed with fresh peppermint leaves.

We had tea on a small white table right out in the courtyard, in the shade of one of the orange trees. Ed's servant, Habiba, came out to serve the tea as well as some tasty cookies made in the shapes of hearts, birds and moons. Habiba had the friendliest, kindest face Beth had seen in a long, long time. She was around fifty and had very beautiful eyes. She bowed slightly upon seeing us and put her hand

14

to her breast, shook each of our hands and then kissed her own—as if to say she was honored to have shaken our hands.

"That's how they say 'howdy' 'round these parts," Ed explained. "Now where's that cunnin' little niece of mine scurried off to? Pamela-Ann!" he called in a loud voice. "Pamela-Ann! You mosey on down here and say howdy to our guests!"

"I had no idea you had family staying with you," said our dad. "I hope we won't be too big a burden on you."

"None at all," Ed responded. "Always glad to be hospitable. Besides, it's the least I can do for someone who's doin' so much for me! And anyway, my Pamela-Ann is just a few years younger than your Beth. Dollars to doughnuts they'll be best friends in no time!"

"Or so we may hope," murmured Granny Bea as though she'd read Beth's mind. "Now where is this niece of yours?"

"I don't rightly know," Ed answered. "Pamela-Ann!" he shouted. "Pamela-Ann! Come down this very minute!"

"No!" came the whiny reply a moment later. "I won't!"

"Pamela-Ann's in a bit of a bad temper," Ed explained. "You see, my brother—Pamela-Ann's father—and his wife have gone wilderness camping. So they sent Pamela-Ann here for the summer. I enrolled Pamela-Ann in a French course, but so far she's refused to go. I declare she must be lonesome for Texas, where we all come from. Pamela-Ann! Where are you? I said c'mon down!"

"Are there cookies?" the whiny voice asked.

"There sure are," answered Ed, "and I advise you to hurry on down before the last one is gone!"

We then heard the loud stomping of feet along the balcony overhead and moments later Pamela-Ann appeared, trotting at a quick clip. She was definitely on the plump side and her long thick pigtails streamed behind her as she ran. At the bottom of the stairs she paused to give a doll's baby carriage standing there a swift kick before dashing up to the table.

Her narrow eyes were shining with pleasure as she eyed the basket filled with cookies. A pudgy hand darted out and grabbed as many cookies as it could hold. Seconds later, all the hearts and moons were thrown back in the basket and Pamela-Ann started downing the bird-shaped ones she had kept. She bit the heads off the bird-cookies and then ate the bodies. When she had finished six, Pamela-Ann looked in Teasdale's direction and said:

"He's sitting in *my* chair! *I* want him off! *I* want to sit down!"

"Teasdale," our dad started to say, "why don't you just give Pam her chair? You and Leo can share."

"*My* name's not Pam, it's Pamela-Ann!" the pudgy nine-year-old informed our dad. She then turned to Teasdale and said, "You heard what your father said—now get off my chair!"

Teasdale was getting paler by the second when our granny cleared her throat, glared icily at Pamela-Ann, and said: "Young lady, I will thank you to retain at least a semblance of courtesy toward the guests in your uncle's house, where, need I remind you, you are yourself a guest! However, your whining is for naught. *We* have finished our tea, and quite a delicious one it was too, and now I plan to read for a while. I am sure your uncle and my son have business to discuss. As for my grandchildren, I plan on giving them each a small sum of money and setting them loose until lunch in the Djemaa el Fna, where no doubt they shall have a most entertaining hour or so. Thus you shall have *all* the chairs! I trust you shall enjoy them in solitude—those with ill manners are often left alone!"

16

"Now, Miss Bea," Ed began, "my little Pamela-Ann is far from her kin . . ."

"She is also far from a proper standard of politeness!" interrupted our granny. "The matter is closed!"

In silence we were given a total of twenty dirhams, which was around five dollars, and told to be careful and have fun.

"Don't be gone long, y'hear," said Ed. "My English partners are coming for one of Habiba's lunches. Lordy, can that gal cook! They should be here in about an hour. Now, James," he went on, "about those loans . . ."

Pamela-Ann was soon left alone to ponder what Granny Bea had said. Beth wasn't sure if the message had penetrated that spoiled skull, but one thing was sure: Pamela-Ann spelled trouble!

Chapter III

Daniel in Distress

Once we'd made our way back to the Djemaa el Fna, we decided to separate and meet in half an hour and then do something together.

Beth spent her half hour wandering among the crowd and watching all the strange things. The best thing she saw was a trained donkey who smoked a cigarette and then pretended to get sick. Leo met an old storyteller who could speak some English and the two traded stories about martians.

In fact, Beth and Leo got so involved in what they were doing, we both managed to be late to meet Teasdale. We found our poet brother in the appointed meeting place, sitting on a wooden bench, holding an empty bag and crying his eyes out.

"I'm sorry we're late," began Beth. "But you see Leo and I were—"

"I am not crying because you're late," Teasdale answered, "but because of cruel, cruel fate!"

"Cruel who?" asked Leo."

"Cruel fate," repeated Teasdale. "It's something that is not very kind or great." Teasdale would say no more but asked us to do something a little unusual. He wanted us to follow him to a certain spot and scream as though our very lives depended on it. He wouldn't tell us why, just that it was extremely important. We've known Teasdale long enough not to be especially surprised by anything he does or says, so we agreed and followed him through the crowd.

He led us past old ladies in veils selling baskets, past children in rags selling hard-boiled eggs, past booths selling the long robes called *"djellabas"* everyone in Morocco wears, and up to another large ring of people watching something we couldn't yet see.

"Count to ten," said Teasdale, "and when you're through, start to scream for a minute or two."

He disappeared, and while we were counting, we peered through the crowd and saw a small man in a turban surrounded by at least ten performing monkeys. They were especially pretty little monkeys, with soft intelligent faces and sad, sad eyes. Even Leo, who can go for months without washing his hands, noticed how dirty and ill-kempt these monkeys were. Each wore a tight collar with a heavy chain leading to the hand of their keeper. The keeper's other hand was on a long stick with which he would occasionally hit one of the monkeys—and hard, too. But the saddest thing of all was a tiny baby monkey, crammed into a cage the size of a small shoe-box. His mournful little face was peeking out from behind the bars, just as though he were remembering the jungle he had come from—if that was where he had come from. Beth is no expert on where monkeys live and neither is Leo.

One thing we did know was that his tiny prison hadn't been cleaned in a good long time.

"I've got to ten," announced Leo and started howling. Beth joined him, and as we both have extremely strong voices in no time at all the people had stopped looking at the monkeys and were looking at us.

It was beginning to get slightly embarrassing when Teasdale appeared, still carrying his paper bag which by now seemed to have something in it.

"Let's get out of here," he whispered urgently, "and do so while the coast is clear."

Teasdale refused to tell us what was in the bag, but Beth started to have a good idea when she saw the bag wiggle once or twice. She began to have a better idea when Teasdale stopped at a fruit stand and bought enough bananas to feed New Jersey.

"They're for Habiba," he said. "She told me they were good to eat. In fact, she said they're quite a treat!"

"Hmmm," responded Beth suspiciously, as she watched the paper bag continue to wiggle.

We found our way back to the house, Teasdale clutching his mysterious package and Beth carrying the bananas. The door was opened by Habiba who kissed us on both cheeks and said something in Arabic.

Teasdale reached into his pocket with his free hand and pulled out a rather crumpled flower which he gave to Habiba.

"Je te donne cette fleur," he said in French, *"parce que tu as un gentil coeur."* (Translated, this means Teasdale was giving Habiba the flower because she had a kind heart.)

Habiba beamed at Teasdale, patted him gently on the head, looked at the bag and winked.

Up in his and Leo's room, Teasdale opened the paper bag and out leapt the baby monkey. He gave a great bound and in no time at all was swinging from the overhead light. Suddenly he was across the room hiding under the bed. The next second he had overturned the wastepaper basket and was throwing its contents in the air like confetti.

"Teasdale!" said Beth sternly. "Of all the—"

"Yeah!" agreed Leo. "How'll we keep this little guy hidden from our dad and Granny Bea?"

"Not to mention Pamela-Ann!" added Beth ominously.

"Oh, Daniel's as well-behaved as me or you," replied Teasdale. "He does just what I tell him to."

"Why Daniel?" we wanted to know.

Teasdale then explained that he'd named the baby monkey after Daniel in the Bible, the one who was rescued from the den of angry lions.

"I didn't see any lions—" began Leo earnestly while Teasdale showed us that Daniel really was well-behaved.

For example, Teasdale clapped his hands once and Daniel stopped dead in his tracks and was perfectly silent; Teasdale clapped twice and Daniel started leaping around as usual. Don't ask me how Teasdale was able to tame the monkey so quickly. I'd guess it had something to do with the monkey being so happy to be rescued that he decided to do exactly what his rescuer told him.

Of course we petted Daniel like crazy and told him he was the cutest monkey we'd ever seen. We also told Teasdale he was the naughtiest boy we'd ever seen and how bad it was to steal. Later in the day, Beth sneaked off to the Djemaa el Fna and when no one was looking dropped a large amount of money in the monkey-man's basket so it would seem more as though Teasdale had bought Daniel, not stolen him.

While we were waiting for lunch we explored the house. Leo found Ed Greyley's study which contained a home computer linked up to the main office of Ed's company. Leo, who had taken a course in computer science the previous spring, started fiddling around with the machine.

He was interested to know exactly how much allowance he'd receive over the next ten years. Only the week before, Leo had asked our dad to give him ten years' allowance at one time. Leo said that since it was going to be his money anyway, he should be getting interest on it too. Our dad had

21

replied that he wouldn't consider such a silly idea, but the least Leo could do would be to come up with some concrete figures.

Leo had just typed in the information to figure out his allowance for one year—fifty-two times two dollars, plus the seventy-five cents he earns per week for bringing in the morning paper—and was shocked to read on the printout the grand total of one thousand, four hundred and thirty dollars!"

"I'm rich!" he shouted before realizing something was wrong. "Hmm," he murmured, "I must have made a mistake. My answer's just about ten times bigger than it should be!"

At this moment, however, our dad and Ed Greyley appeared in the study door.

"Leo G. Smith!" exclaimed our dad from the door. "What on earth are you up to?"

Ed Greyley didn't wait to find out. He raced across the room and fairly snatched Leo away from the computer.

"The kid could erase everything!" he explained. "This machine is linked up to the records at the main office! Heaven knows what would happen if he messed up my inventories!"

"But I'm a computer expert, at least I thought I was," said Leo, rubbing the shoulder that Greyley had grabbed when pulling him away from the computer.

"I'm sure the boy meant no harm," said our dad.

"Of course not," replied Ed Greyley, slightly embarrassed. "I sure 'nuff didn't mean to jump on the boy—I just had no way of knowin' he knew all about computers. Now what was it you were tryin' to figure out?"

Leo explained and Greyley, after fiddling with a knob or two, showed Leo how to operate the computer correctly, and in no time at all Leo came up with the correct answer—

though needless to say our dad told him to forget the whole idea.

"Even though you might be a computer expert," Ed told Leo after our dad had vetoed Leo's suggestion, "I sure would be grateful if you wouldn't horse around with this here computer without my permission."

"I won't do it again," said Leo as the front-door knocker sounded, announcing the arrival of the Hodgsons, Ed Greyley's business partners.

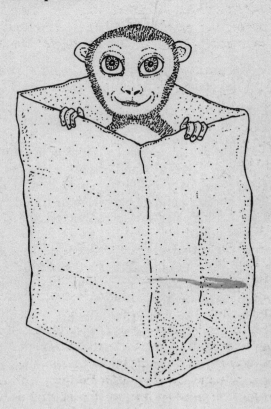

Chapter IV

A Silver Tea Server and a Yellow Citroën

"It is most horribly hot outside today," announced Lady Cynthia Hodgson as she and her husband, Lord Lionel, stepped into the shade of the orange trees in Ed Greyley's courtyard.

"You said it, m'am," agreed Ed. "I declare it's hotter than Texas!"

Lady Hodgson was an elegant woman in her thirties. She spoke with British perfection and had not a hair out of place. The dress she wore was made of hand-sewn lace and the jewels around her neck and on her wrists sparkled brilliantly. Her eyes were blue, her lips red, but on the whole her expression was cold.

Lord Hodgson, also elegantly dressed, seemed much friendlier. His grey eyes sparkled as much as his wife's jewels and his cheeks were rosy from the sun while his wife's were pale and white.

"Awfully kind of you to come all this way to assist in our business transactions," he said to our dad after the introductions had been made.

"Glad to help," replied our dad modestly. "And besides, I've always wanted to see Morocco."

"Quite, quite," murmured Lord Hodgson as we sat down

to Habiba's delicious lunch. Even Pamela-Ann seemed pleased by the salad of tomatoes and green peppers cooked Moroccan-style, the fried eggplant dish and the enormous *cous-cous* (which is a grain served with chick peas, all kinds of vegetables, and a scrumptious gravy).

For side dishes there were bowls of salted almonds, dried dates and apricots, and a soup we couldn't identify. And there was tons of bread which the Moroccans like to eat with everything.

Dessert consisted of some delicious cakes followed by yogurt and mint tea, served Moroccan-style out of a pretty silver tea server.

"Nasty stuff," remarked Lady Hodgson on the subject of the mint tea. "Why they call it tea is simply beyond comprehension! How I long for a good English cup of tea! And out of a good old-fashioned brown teapot—like the one I had when I was a girl, not one of these silver jobbies!"

"Now, now, dear," soothed Lord Hodgson; "It really is most frightfully good once you get used to it."

"I prefer Coca-Cola," stated Pamela-Ann. "But at home my mother won't let me drink it. She says it rots your teeth."

"And quite right she is too," said Granny Bea as she sipped her mint tea.

"By the way," said Lord Hodgson, "have you heard the latest news? It's bloody depressing."

"No," Ed replied, "what's up?"

"There's been another kidnapping, and just this morning," Lord Hodgson replied. He then explained that there had been a string of kidnappings terrorizing the wealthier residents of Marrakech for over six months. "Thank heaven all the children have been returned unharmed!" he added.

"And," Lord Hodgson continued, "the kidnappers have been asking the most awesome sums of money. There can be no doubt someone is getting awfully rich from all this!"

"What a disgrace!" snorted our granny. "I knew this part of the world was unsafe! Can the police do nothing to stop this unlawful rampage?"

"The police!" laughed Ed Greyley. "I've met the Chief of Police, and I don't think he could find a cow in a kitchen!"

"Actually," said Lord Hodgson to our granny, "Marrakech is surprisingly crime-free. Believe it or not, its crime rate is much lower than some European or American cities of a similar size."

"Tell it to the Marines!" declared Granny Bea.

"Who got it this time?" demanded Pamela-Ann merrily.

"Got what, little niece?"

"Kidnapped, of course," answered Pamela-Ann.

"Merciful heavens!" snapped Granny Bea. "I do not find kidnapping a matter for amusement!"

"Unless you get kidnapped by martians on a UFO!" put in Leo excitedly. "That's the dream of my life!"

"Well," continued Lord Hodgson, "apparently it was little Arielle Dorléac. I happen to know the child—only twelve, and a dear girl too."

"How dreadful!" said our Granny. "And where did this misdeed occur?"

"At the airport. It seems Arielle was returning from visiting relatives in France and the kidnappers met her at the airport, forced her into a car and that was the last anyone has seen or heard from her—aside from the ransom note, of course. These devils make the poor children write the notes themselves!"

"You seem to know an ungodly amount about this sordid business, dear," commented Lady Hodgson. "From what I understood, the police have been refusing to release any details concerning these cases to avoid public panic."

"I happen to have had tea with an associate of Arielle's father," Lord Hodgson explained, "and he told me all about it. But the good part is they think they've got a lead, slight though it may be."

"A lead, did you say?" inquired Lady Hodgson.

"Tell us, man. What is it?" demanded Ed Greyley.

"Apparently some tourists at the airport thought they witnessed the kidnapping. Two claimed they could identify the make of car used, but unfortunately they couldn't agree on what color it was."

"I don't suppose it happened to be a Citroën," said Leo in a quiet voice.

"However did you know?"

"Because we saw it too!" burst out Beth. "And it was yellow!"

"What was yellow?" wondered Ed Greyley.

"The Citroën, of course," replied Beth and Leo in unison.

"That's not fair!" whined Pamela-Ann. "They got to see a kidnapping and I didn't!"

A knock on the door interrupted Pamela-Ann's complaints and soon a young Moroccan man around twenty-five years old entered the courtyard. He was slim and well-dressed, his black hair combed back from his forehead revealing intelligent eyes. He was Jalil Khaldouni, an employee of the Hodgsons and Ed Greyley, and apparently a bright young man. He was fluent in Arabic, French and English, and also a whiz with computers.

"Here are the papers you required, sir," he said to Ed Greyley, bowed, and left via the kitchen where we could hear him speaking rapid Arabic to Habiba.

"I don't trust that young man," said Ed in a low voice. "He's always hanging around here, nosing about with my computer, talking with Habiba, and who knows what else!"

"I quite agree," nodded Lady Hodgson. "And just consider how well-dressed he always is. How he affords such elegant attire on what we pay him is impossible to imagine!"

"Really, my dear," chuckled Lord Hodgson affectionately, "you're hardly the one to speak! It's not for nothing you're known as the best-dressed woman in Marrakech! And how you do it on our limited budget I'll—"

"I beg your pardon for interrupting this most illuminating discussion," said our granny in a loud voice, "but it appears to me we have important information concerning this latest kidnapping which I feel should be conveyed posthaste to the police!"

"Of course, little lady!" smiled Ed Greyley, "not that it'll do much good!"

"Whether or not it does good can hardly be considered my responsibility," replied Granny Bea primly. "I simply feel it is my duty to assist the police whenever possible, no matter how incompetent they may be."

"Well said!" cheered Lord Hodgson. "I'll have our chauffeur pop you 'round to Police Headquarters directly as lunch is over."

"And we'll go with you!" urged Beth. "After all, Teasdale, Leo, and I were eyewitnesses! I bet the Chief'll be dying to talk with us!"

"More likely he'll be dying to go home and take a nap!" Lady Hodgson remarked cynically.

Police Headquarters was located in the new part of Marrakech, known as the Guéliz after some small hills bordering it. The Guéliz was extremely modern and attractive, the streets were wide and tree-lined, the sidewalks swept and dotted with charming cafés, and the shops all had bright elegant displays. The buildings were tall and mostly in the same shades of pink and ochre as in the old part of town.

"Hmmph," said Granny Bea as she viewed the scene through the windows of the Hodgsons' chauffeured Jaguar, "this is actually a good deal better-looking than a number of American cities it has been my misfortune to visit."

28

"Yeah," agreed Leo, "and that big tall building straight ahead would be perfect for a UFO landing! Besides, it hardly ever rains here. I don't think UFOs like rain!"

"No rain," considered Beth, "and warm all year . . . Just think, the baseball season need never end!"

"With walls of pink and skies of blue, this is the perfect place for me and you," rhymed Teasdale thoughtfully. But I don't think he would have thought it so perfect if he'd known what lay in store. . . .

"The Chief of Police will see you now," said a secretary, and we were ushered into a bare modern office overlooking the main street in the Guéliz.

Moustafa Beljhazi, the Chief of Police, looked up from the comic book he'd been reading, frowned, and asked, "How may I you assist?"

"We wish to offer evidence of the utmost importance concerning the kidnapping of Arielle Dorléac," announced our grandmother in a loud voice.

"But yes," said Moustafa (whom we started calling Moustacha on account of the funny little mustache that was perched just above his lips). "Thank you very much and good-bye!"

"Good-bye?" said Beth. "But we haven't told you anything yet!"

"No?" said Moustacha. "Then do so, if you please."

So we told him. His thin brown face wrinkled slightly as he listened.

"No," he said when we had finished. "This information, it is not very aiding at all."

"I beg your pardon!" snorted Granny Bea. "I find it extremely 'aiding,' as you call it."

"My dear madam," Moustacha replied, "have you the smallest idea as to how many yellow Citroëns there may be in Marrakech? I doubt I could even count them!"

"I doubt you can even count!" said Beth, though under her breath so only Teasdale and Leo could hear.

29

"But that's not right!" countered Leo. "I watched all the way over from where we were staying and I only saw two Citroëns of that kind of model—the 2–CV—and neither of them was bright yellow! I think it must be a very rare car!"

"Evidently," agreed Moustacha with a smile. "It is so rare I think we have no hope of finding it!"

"Merciful heavens!" commented Granny Bea as we glided home among the busy streets in the Jaguar. "That man has about as much sense as Pamela-Ann!"

"Yes," agreed Teasdale, "and if all the police here are as stupid as he, Marrakech is not a good place to kidnapped be!"

Truer words were never spoken!

Chapter V

Quiet Footsteps Up a Dark Stairway

"Christopher Columbus!" exclaimed Beth after we'd returned to Ed Greyley's. "With that Moustacha guy in charge of the police, that poor kid they kidnapped will never get rescued!"

"That's for sure!" agreed Leo. "Boy, do I feel sorry for her!"

"So do I," Beth went on, "but not for long!"

"What do you mean 'not for long'?" Leo wondered.

"I mean once we rescue her we won't have to feel sorry for her," explained Beth.

"Rescue her!" gasped Leo.

"Of course," Beth replied. "It's up to us to save that poor Arielle!"

So the following morning Beth and Leo set out to see what they could find, each of them going a separate way and keeping a sharp lookout for the Citroën 2-CV. Teasdale announced that he was going to take Daniel for a stroll through the public gardens and then out shopping to replenish the diminished banana supply.

Beth's morning was not productive. She enjoyed exploring the maze of streets that make up the old part of town, getting entirely lost only to discover herself back in the exact place from which she'd started. Marrakech was a very

31

secret kind of place—whether it was the tiny wooden doors hiding lovely homes like Ed Greyley's, or the still beggars, draped in grey, and hidden to the world save for a gnarled hand outstretched to receive money. And there were cats everywhere—leaping from rooftop to rooftop, darting underfoot, watching silently from the shadows or purring and washing themselves in the sun. Beth also saw two large storks winging their way across the blue Moroccan sky, far above the stately mosques that tower above the pink city.

Beth had just found her way back to the Greyley place where, at the little wooden door, she met Leo, only that second returned from his investigations. He was puffing with excitement and all red in the face.

"It was better than seeing a UFO!" he exclaimed.

"What was better?" Beth wanted to know.

"I found the Citroën!" boasted Leo. "But that's not all! Come inside and I'll tell you the rest!"

Up in Beth's room Leo resumed his story:

"I was walking around the Djemaa el Fna when I happened to see the yellow Citroën driving toward the big parking lot on the far side. So I raced over and was able to trail the guy who had been driving it. He walked first to a small building with a restaurant on the ground floor that looked really dirty and awful. He went in through a side-door and up a stairway that seemed to lead to apartments above the restaurant. About two minutes later he came back out, looking pleased, and holding a piece of paper in his hand. Now here comes the weird part—he went back to the Djemaa el Fna and put the piece of paper into the snake charmer's basket!"

"Ugh!" said Beth. "What a place to leave a message! What happened next?"

"I'm afraid I lost him," admitted Leo. "He got in the Citroën and drove off so quickly he almost ran over two tourists. Anyway, he left so fast I couldn't even tell which direction he went."

"Hmmm," said Beth. "Good work, Leo. Thanks to you we know a lot: We know where their hideout is and we know how they pass messages to each other! Boy," continued Beth, "won't Teasdale be interested in all this. It's so weird and mysterious he'll probably want to write a poem about it!"

But lunchtime came and went and Teasdale hadn't returned. We wondered if perhaps he'd been sighted by Daniel's previous owner and carted off to prison for monkeynapping. We also couldn't help but wonder if maybe the worst had happened—that Teasdale had been kidnapped. But no one wanted to even mention such a thing. No one, that is, except for Pamela-Ann.

"He's probably been kidnapped," she whined. "And serve him right too for not giving me back my chair yesterday when I asked him to!"

"Bite your tongue, young lady!" reprimanded our granny in a sharp voice.

Then at three o'clock came some good news: Arielle Dorléac, the kidnapped French girl, had been released unharmed after her parents paid the kidnappers an enormous ransom.

So the afternoon dragged on; we were all so worried we couldn't do anything useful. Finally, as you already know, came the dreadful letter telling us Teasdale had been kidnapped.

As we all gathered around Teasdale's note and the message from the kidnappers, Leo noticed something unusual about Teasdale's signature:

"Look!" he cried. "Poor Teasdale! He must have been so nervous he capitalized the 'S' in the middle of his name!"

"I don't think it's a mistake," Beth said, reading over

Leo's shoulder. "I bet the 'S' is a clue of some kind!"

Our dad went off to break the news to our granny, and Ed Greyley called the Chief of Police.

"It's a bad business," Ed told our dad, "but don't worry too much. I'm sure everything'll come out just fine."

"That's right," agreed Lady Hodgson, who'd dropped by to deliver some papers. "And remember, none of the kidnapped children have been harmed, and that's what counts."

Mr. Moustacha arrived half an hour later. He was not pleased to have had his afternoon nap interrupted and seemed even less pleased to see Granny Bea a second time.

"Have you more aiding to me give?" he asked.

"As it happens, I do not," our granny responded. "Unfortunately we have called you here on a matter of the utmost urgency. My young grandson, Teasdale Smith, has been foully kidnapped."

Granny Bea then started to cry, something she very rarely allows herself to do.

Moustacha listened attentively while our dad explained the situation.

"Ah!" Moustacha said. "I understand what has happened to the young monsieur!"

"You do?" we gasped.

"But of course," he replied. "Evidently he has been kidnapped!"

Mr. Moustacha left half an hour later after promising to do all he could to find our lost brother, but it was difficult to have much confidence in someone like him.

It really was terrible. Our dad was sitting stunned in a chair, saying nothing, just staring straight ahead like a zombie; and our granny had been helped to her bed, complaining of pains around her heart. Pamela-Ann was upstairs taking a very loud bath and singing to herself in an ugly off-tune voice while her uncle was wandering around trying to be

34

cheerful. He said everything would be all right so many times that Beth was ready to punch him. Habiba took the news hard, being as fond of Teasdale as he was of her. Beth could hear her in the kitchen quietly crying.

Beth and Leo were probably the most upset of all. Teasdale may be a little strange but we both love him all the more for it. Since our mom died a few years ago, we three kids have always done everything together, especially since our dad's business takes him away from home a lot. So we three kids have learned how to take care of each other.

So we didn't waste a second in our attempts to locate Teasdale. The minute our dad turned his back and Ed Greyley went off to fiddle with his computer, with Habiba still weeping in the kitchen and Pamela-Ann still singing in the bath, we sneaked out the door—bound for the little building Leo had seen the man enter that afternoon.

A happy surprise was waiting for us just outside the door of Ed Greyley's—there was Daniel! He looked a bit worse for wear and his eyes had the saddest expression. We imagined he must have been missing Teasdale as much as we were. Too bad he couldn't tell us where Teasdale was!

When we got to the building it was past nine o'clock and night had fallen. The bustling streets were washed with blue shadows, and the passersby, dark silhouettes in long robes with pointed hoods, cast eerie shadows as they seemed to glide by.

We tiptoed past the brightly lit restaurant with its blaring Arab music and loudly conversing customers, entered a dark doorway and silently mounted a pitch-black stairway, so dark we had to feel our way along the crumbling wall.

Up and further up we went, feeling our way the whole time, almost too scared to breathe. It was utterly quiet and completely black. We climbed until at last we found ourselves in a hallway, lit only by a street lamp shining through a dirty window.

There were only two doors opening onto the hallway, so we tiptoed toward the closest, and putting our ears next to it could hear a baby crying and a mother cooing. Somehow a cooing mother didn't fit our idea of a kidnapper, so we proceeded to the next.

No sound issued from the far side of the door—just a horrible silence.

Summoning all her courage, Beth tried the knob, but the door was locked. Next she knocked, but there was no answer.

Beth looked at Leo, and Leo looked at Beth. Beth raised her eyebrows and nodded questioningly in the direction of the door. Leo narrowed his eyes in thought and then nodded back in silent response.

Without a word, we took a step back from the door, squared our shoulders the way we'd learned in football practice, and charged.

The lock groaned, the wood splintered and the door gave way, sending us flying into the room and tumbling onto the floor. It was lucky for us no one was there waiting for us, since it took us a minute or two to regain our feet, not to mention our bearings.

Even by the dim light of the street lamp we could see the room was empty. Secretly we both had been nursing the hope that we'd find Teasdale here and the whole horrible nightmare would be over as quickly as it had started.

Leo lit some matches and started looking for clues. The quivering light went slowly from room to room, with Beth walking solemnly alongside it.

It turned out to be a fair-sized apartment, with four rooms and a bath. In a small room to the left of the bathroom we found a pile of odd-smelling wooden boxes. They were small and beautifully made of a dark grainy wood. The best thing about them was the top: It was held in place without nails or hinges, but by the pressure of the box's sides. You had to force the top open by pressing hard with your thumb, and once open, it seemed just the right size to put matches in. We looked through all of the boxes and they were all empty. Beth took one just in case they might turn out to be important evidence.

It was in the last and smallest room that we found our final clues. For there, in the crack in the floor, was hidden Teasdale's sterling silver writing pen our uncle had sent him from London. We both knew it was one of Teasdale's most treasured possessions and we realized how painful it must have been for Teasdale to part with it.

"I bet it was all he had to leave behind to show he'd been here," said Beth, brushing a tear from her eye. Beth isn't the kind of girl to spend her time crying, but just imagining our brother being held prisoner in that horrible dirty little room in that awful house was more than she could take. Suddenly she wanted to get out of that filthy prison, so she ran toward the door.

"Beth!" Leo called. "Come back! I've found something!"

Walking slowly back into the little room, Beth found Leo crouched down in the corner, a lighted match held up near the wall. Bending down beside her brother, Beth could just make out something scrawled in a great hurry on the wall, but still in our brother's particular script:

It was the letter "S."

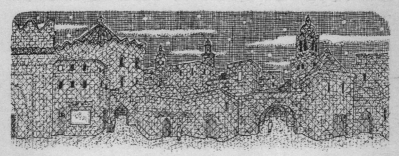

Chapter VI

An Important Box and an Ugly Baby

The Djemaa el Fna was deserted at dawn. Aside from us there were only five or six people in sight, mostly sad homeless ones with nowhere to go. The first glimmer of light was inching over the mountains surrounding Marrakech and the prayers wailed from the mosques indicated it was five o'clock, the hour for the morning prayer.

The bus terminal was also dark, with only a small lighted window where we bought our tickets. The ticket seller directed us toward a bus, parked at the rear of the cavernous garage where the fleet of buses stood, all awaiting departures for various points around Morocco.

The air in the terminal was so foul with exhaust fumes Leo tried holding his breath until the bus left, which of course was impossible, because it wasn't due to leave for another twenty minutes. We kept Daniel happy by keeping him fed with a steady stream of bananas. We'd also brought along Pamela-Ann's doll's baby carriage, all folded up, in case we needed to put Daniel in it to keep him out of sight.

Our bus was already packed with people. It was a regular-sized bus, but somehow they had put in at least thirty extra seats, and each of these seemed to hold at least two Moroccans.

At last the driver materialized, drinking a cup of very black coffee and scratching his stubbled chin. He pulled a key out from the depths of his long brown and grey robe, threw the half-empty cup out the bus window, started the engine and we were off.

"I wonder what Essaouira's like," mused Beth as the bus pulled away from the terminal and into the pale light of early morning—for it was to a town called Essaouira that we were bound. . . .

Things had happened quickly after our discovery of the kidnappers' hideout. First of all, our dad and our granny were furious with us.

"You are shockingly naughty children for sneaking off!" our granny told us.

"And that's not all," continued our dad. "Don't you realize how dangerous a caper that was? What if the kidnappers had been there? Just think what could have happened!"

Even Ed Greyley got into the action: "You are foolish little children!" he said in a harsh voice. "Only a foolish child would go snooping around in a foreign city! If I were your father I'd give you a spanking you'd never forget!"

"You know," said Beth to Leo after we'd been sent upstairs in disgrace, "maybe that Ed Greyley isn't as nice as he acts!"

"I don't know. . . ." considered Leo. "Maybe he was just really worried that we might have been hurt."

Only Habiba seemed pleased by what we had done. We knew this because after we'd been sent upstairs she silently appeared with some delicious Moroccan pastries to cheer us up. To thank her Leo gave her the box we'd found at the kidnappers even though Beth said that was no way to handle important evidence.

While we were busy downing Habiba's pastries, the grown-ups were busy talking in fast urgent voices. We heard Ed Greyley make a number of phone calls, sometimes talking in English and sometimes in French. Before long Moustacha had come and gone, spouting nonsense about our information concerning the kidnappers' hideout not being very aiding. Granny Bea got so mad she gave him a swift bat with her swan-head umbrella that we thought would surely knock off his mustache.

Jalil Khaldouni also appeared with a message from one of the Hodgsons. We heard Ed Greyley telling him all about the kidnapping, and peering over the balcony we saw Jalil shaking his head about the news—though it seemed to us more in anger than surprise.

Jalil then bid Ed Greyley and our dad goodnight, and left via the kitchen where he had a brief but animated chat with Habiba. Even though they spoke in Arabic we knew they were discussing the kidnapping because we heard Teasdale's name spoken again and again.

Ed Greyley was still saying not to worry, no harm would come to Teasdale, when our dad announced he was going to bed. Granny Bea was already asleep, having taken a sedative, but Pamela-Ann was singing along to the radio.

At last Ed Greyley told his niece to quiet down and silence fell over the unhappy house. Beth was sleeping in Leo's room so he wouldn't have to be alone. Just as we were getting into our pajamas we heard a soft knock on the door.

Slowly the door opened and in walked Habiba carrying a book, with her finger on her lips telling us to keep quiet. In silence she opened the book on the bed and pointed at it meaningfully.

It was a guidebook to Morocco, written in English. For a moment Beth thought Habiba had chosen an odd time to give us a lesson about tourist sights in Morocco. Then she followed the direction of Habiba's finger. And there, on the left-hand page, was a photograph of the same sort of box we'd found at the kidnappers' and had given to Habiba!

Taking the book in her hands, Beth read the caption below the photo out loud so Leo could hear:

"'This box is a charming example of but one of many wooden objects handmade from the roots of trees. The largest center of craftsmen working with such wood is in the delightful seaside town of Essaouira.'"

"Essaouira!" repeated Habiba urgently.

"Essaouira . . ." said Beth thoughtfully.

"Hey!" exclaimed Leo. "It begins with an 'S' sound, even though it's spelled with an 'E'! That must have been what Teasdale was trying to tell us in his note!"

"Christopher Columbus!" Beth shouted. "That's it! That explains the 'S' on the wall and the capital 'S' in the note! They must have taken Teasdale to Essaouira!"

Using sign language, Beth pointed toward herself and Leo, and then toward a picture of Essaouira in the guidebook.

"Oui, Essaouira!" replied Habiba, clapping her hands as her watchful face relaxed into a broad smile. She then made a sound imitating a bus and pointing toward Leo's wristwatch, she reached out, took the watch and changed the time to five-thirty.

"She must mean there's a bus at five-thirty that goes to Essaouira!" said Leo excitedly. "But from where? Oh, I wish Habiba spoke English—or we spoke French or Arabic!"

Again using sign language, Beth indicated to Habiba she wanted to know where the bus left from.

"Djemaa el Fna," replied Habiba, leaving the room as silently as she had come in.

So the next morning, as quietly as thieves, we left Ed Greyley's house on Derb el Hammam and found our way to the bus terminal right off the Djemaa el Fna.

So they wouldn't worry too much, or think we'd been kidnapped too, we left our dad and Granny a note:

"Dear Dad and Granny Bea,

We have gone to find Teasdale. We will be very careful and will return when we have found him. We think we know where he is.

Love,

Beth and Leo

P.S. We had to borrow a bit of money from Dad's wallet. Hope you don't mind."

By the time the sun was high in the sky we were chugging through the flat plains west of Marrakech, heading toward the ocean.

As the crowded old bus rattled along, and Daniel started getting a bit restless, Beth started to worry.

"Leo," she said, "do you think we're doing the right thing?"

"What do you mean?"

"I mean are we sure Habiba's right? Why would the kidnappers have all those boxes?"

"Maybe since they have to go to Essaouira all the time to hide kidnapped kids, they figured they'd sell boxes on the side," ventured Leo. "Or maybe it's just a cover."

"Good thinking," said Beth. "But there's something more: It's that Habiba seems nice and all, but what if she's in with the kidnappers? Maybe she's just luring us to Essaouira so we can be kidnapped too!"

"I don't think so, Beth," replied Leo as he fed Daniel his forty-ninth banana of the trip. "I think if there's one person we can trust, besides our dad and Granny of course, it would be Habiba."

"I guess you're right," agreed Beth, "but there's something else that keeps nagging at me."

"You mean Pamela-Ann?"

"Besides her, I mean, who knows we're in Marrakech?"

"Lots of people," answered Leo. "Why should that bug you?"

"I mean for Teasdale to have been kidnapped, it just had to have been by someone who knows us. It's not as though we're staying at some big fancy hotel or we're famous or anything. Whoever kidnapped Teasdale just had to know where we're staying and that our dad is rich. And the way I see it, only someone who knew us well would know all that the day after we arrived!"

"Unless it was the taxidriver," suggested Leo thoughtfully.

"Possibly," considered Beth, "except he didn't look smart enough to figure out a kidnapping—I mean a whole string of kidnappings. . . . And besides, he'd have no way of knowing our dad's so rich. No, according to my thinking, the person behind all this could only be Ed Greyley, Jalil, or the Hodgsons!"

"What about Moustacha?"

"Him!" laughed Beth. "I don't think he could plan a trip to the corner, much less a kidnapping!"

"I have to agree," Leo told her. "But we'll have plenty of time to figure out all this later. Let's just concentrate on rescuing Teasdale," he added, as the bus rolled at last into Essaouira.

Essaouira was a pretty little town with white buildings with blue or yellow trim. According to our guidebook it was a fishing village on the Atlantic, just over one hundred miles west of Marrakech. On one side it featured a lively port with fishermen bringing in their hauls and on the other a huge fortress, built long ago by the Portuguese. The fortress was full of cannons and turrets and small secret chambers once used for storing ammunition. These were now used as workshops for local woodworkers, which of course was what led us to Essaouira in the first place.

We got off the bus in a large open area near the port. The sky was blue, the air smelled of the sea and everyone we saw smiled at us and said *"La-bess,"* which is how people in Morocco usually say hello.

Our first course of action was to retire to the shade of a palm tree and hold a secret conference.

We'd decided back in Marrakech that just in case the kidnappers were lurking around town, looking out for rescuers, we'd have to do our investigating in disguise. Leo had wanted to disguise us as martians until Beth explained that this would draw more attention to us than was good. What we had to do was fit in.

It was Beth who came up with the idea of disguising ourselves as a Moroccan woman. We'd borrowed one of Habiba's robes, which Beth now put on; with the hood up and a veil over her face, no one would recognize her in a million years. Then Leo got under the robe too. Since he's a good head shorter than Beth, he was hidden completely. Luckily there were a few button holes in front, so Leo could peer through them to see where we were going. Daniel we disguised as a baby by wrapping him in white rags and putting him in Pamela-Ann's doll carriage, which looked sturdy enough to carry Pamela-Ann—and her uncle too!

Thus by the time we left the tree's shade, gone were the two American kids and one Moroccan monkey, and in their place was a veiled and rather oddly shaped Moroccan woman pushing a baby carriage containing a tiny Moroccan baby named Daniel!

Consulting our guidebook as we went along, we gradually headed for the part of Essaouira housing the woodworkers—the old fortress, or the Battlements, as it was called.

It was slow going, for not only were the narrow white-washed streets filled with both Moroccans and tourists, but it was also difficult walking with Leo under the robe—we kept bumping into one another. And Daniel didn't make the world's best-behaved baby—he kept squirming around in his carriage in a most unbabylike manner.

As we neared the Battlements, two tourists approached us. With both horror and amazement, Beth recognized the two middle-aged ladies: They were Miss Abegonia Leach, one of Beth's teachers (and the meanest in the universe), and her sister Louella, Leo's last year's teacher!

The two women walked right over to us, introduced themselves as American schoolteachers, and then Abegonia gave us an enormous smile and said, "Might I snap a picture of you and your baby to show my students back home?"

Beth agreed in a weird-sounding voice, and Abegonia took the photo. Then she reached out with her right hand and patted Daniel on the head.

"What a sweet baby you have!" she said, leaning forward to give our "sweet baby" a kiss, while her sister photographed the pose. But she came into contact not with the smooth soft skin of a baby but with the coarse hairy face of Daniel the monkey! And to make matters worse, Daniel reached out with his paws and tugged at Abegonia's nose! (It did look a bit like a banana.)

"The saints preserve us!" shrieked Abegonia as she leapt back in horror. "That's the most hideous baby I've ever seen!"

She and her sister—who'd also got a glimpse of Daniel's special beauty—turned and fled, screaming all the while.

We meanwhile were also screaming—with laughter. Leo commented it might even be worth having Miss Leach a second year if he could have the chance to see her show his photograph to the class as an example of an authentic Moroccan woman!

"I don't know about that," giggled Beth, "but at least we

do know our disguise would even fool someone who actually knows us!"

The Battlements were absolutely amazing. They consisted of lots of weird turrets overlooking a rocky shore, where surf pounded in on jagged rocks and even the seabirds were afraid to land; wide stone walkways lined with ancient cannons; narrow courtyards and pathways, all built of stone; and last but not least, small dark shops where lovely wooden objects were made and sold.

It was a magical wonderful place, large and intricate, and full of secrets. The air had that special smell of freshly cut wood, and that, mixed with the scent of the sea and the sound of the gulls overhead, held us spellbound.

"Let's keep walking," whispered Beth to Leo, "and look in all the shops until we find the one that sells a box like the one we found. Then maybe we'll find Teasdale!"

"Okay," replied Leo from under the robe.

Off an octagonally shaped courtyard, right under a balcony with a spectacular view of the sea, our search was at last rewarded: In a small shop lit only by a single lantern, we saw a pile of boxes like the ones we'd seen in the apartment!

We entered the dark shop and approached a man bent over a piece of wood near the back, busily sanding. The wind whistled around the little courtyard and the sea pounded nearby.

Then, from the far side of a small door at the back of the little shop, we heard a familiar voice.

"Let me free, you ugly villain!
To be kidnapped, I'm just not willin'!"

We had found what we were looking for. The only question now was how to get it.

But Beth's quick mind was already at work.

"It's now or never!" she whispered. "C'mon, Leo—here we go!"

Chapter VII

Daniel Learns to Fly

Without a sound, Beth emptied a canvas bag she saw lying on a table and on tiptoe she and Leo approached the man working at the back of the shop. Before he knew what had happened, the bag was over his head and shoulders and we had thrown a big piece of rope around him and had tied him to his workbench.

Above the workbench we noticed a key hanging on the wall. Sure enough, this opened a small door at the back of the shop, where a pitiful sight fell upon our eyes.

For there, amidst a pile of old rags, planks of wood, stacks of sandpaper, and yellowed newspapers, sat Teasdale. He was bound hand and foot, his long hair was all dirty, and his face tearstained.

"Unless you've come to set me free, then don't bother speaking to me!" he said, not yet recognizing us.

"Teasdale!" cried Beth. "It's us!"

Teasdale peered in our direction and looked confused. Then Leo wriggled free from under the robe, Beth whipped off her veil, and Daniel, who'd been sitting outside in the baby carriage, darted into the room, making excited monkey noises.

"Beth! Leo! Daniel!" cheered Teasdale as three pairs of hands started untying him. Daniel proved to be an excellent knot-untier.

"How did you find me?" wondered Teasdale as the last rope fell away and Beth was dabbing at some dirt on his face with a moist rag she'd borrowed from the bound man in the shop.

"We'll tell you later," Beth replied. "But now I think we'd better get out of here, and fast—before somebody else shows up!"

"Yes—let's go and never stop! I've spent too long in this old shop!" said Teasdale as we raced out to the street.

"Listen," announced Beth a moment later as we stood on the street, gathered around the baby carriage, "I think Leo and I should keep our costume on—just in case the kidnappers reappear!"

"Oh, but I have no costume," moaned Teasdale. "If they see me, it'll mean certain doom!"

"No it won't," replied Beth, "just hop in the carriage with Daniel—you'll be twins!"

In went Teasdale and off we went.

It was no easy job to push Teasdale and Daniel along the narrow back streets of Essaouira—not because Teasdale weighs a lot, but because Beth and Leo kept knocking into one another under their robe. But we all laughed a lot and felt happy just knowing Teasdale was safe and sound. As we pushed the carriage up a slight hill Beth started telling Teasdale about our encounter with the Misses Leach.

"Sorry to interrupt you, sister most dear," Teasdale said in a quavering voice, "but look behind you and see who's drawing near!"

Beth turned—and saw the man we'd left in the shop. And he had two mean-looking friends with him. And they were heading straight for us. And they didn't look especially happy!

"Achmed, Fatah, and Saïd are their names," explained Teasdale, "and they're not here for playing games!"

We accelerated our pace and so did they. Sweat poured off us as we raced along the street, the baby carriage tilting madly as we rounded corners.

But the kidnappers kept steadily gaining on us as we charged through the busy town. Those kidnappers must practice jogging on their days off! And if we thought walking together in one robe was difficult, well—that was because we'd never tried running! Poor Teasdale was bounced around in the carriage like a ball. Even Daniel, who likes leaping around, had a perplexed unhappy look on his little face.

Arriving at an intersection we had three choices of which way to go. One was a completely black alley that looked positively evil, one was a narrow busy road and the third was even narrower but less crowded. We chose the third and headed down it at a breakneck pace—only to find it was a dead end! It stopped in a little courtyard, with no exit except one rusty hinged door that King Kong wouldn't have been able to open.

Far above us, across the yard, hung a clothesline, but it was too high for us to reach.

We were trapped!

There we stood as the kidnappers arrived, wide yellow smiles shining from the shadows of their hooded faces as they saw they had us cornered.

The three of them stood in the narrow entrance to the courtyard and one said something to us in Arabic that sounded extremely nasty.

Slowly they approached us. The one nearest us reached in his grey robe and pulled out a long sharp sword!

Again he said something to us in Arabic as he took another step toward the baby carriage—and us!

Meanwhile the other two stood on either side of him, holding their gnarled grubby hands out in readiness to start fighting.

We stood there paralyzed. At least Teasdale and Leo were—but not Beth. She had been positive it was the end for us when an interesting thought struck her: Perhaps the kidnappers hadn't recognized us since they were speaking to us in Arabic. Beth imagined they must have thought we were just a Moroccan woman and her baby who for reasons of her own had decided to rescue Teasdale.

"Allah! Allah!" cried Beth in a weird voice.

Once she got the kidnappers' attention, Beth picked up Daniel from the baby carriage he was sharing with Teasdale. She kissed the little fellow as though he really was a baby and she was scared harm might come to him.

Beth kissed Daniel dramatically a few more times, all the while screeching, "Allah! Allah!"—and then she threw Daniel high up in the air, in the direction of the clothesline.

Of course Daniel had no problem grabbing the clothesline and scrambling along it to the wall and from there leaping to the rooftop where he could watch in safety.

And of course the kidnappers, who had no idea that the baby that had just been tossed up in the air like a basektball and who had crawled along the clothesline was really a monkey, stood there with their mouths wide open, in complete shock. And that second of shock enabled us to charge past them and back into the small road and off to freedom!

"Good thinking!" cried Leo from under the robe as we once again were running for our lives, toward the intersection I mentioned earlier.

By the time we got to the intersection, the kidnappers had apparently recovered from the shock of seeing a baby fly through the air and scramble along a wall, and had narrowed our headstart. In fact, Beth could almost smell the foul breath of the one carrying the sword as he galloped close behind her.

Also at the intersection was Daniel, and as we raced through the archway leading to the narrow and busy road in the middle, he leapt from the arch and landed gracefully on Teasdale's head, chattering madly all the while.

This road led past more woodworking shops and up to a small cobblestone street that went up a steep hill to a different part of the Battlements. We could tell it would take us to the section overlooking the sea, and Beth reasoned there probably would be either a lot of tourists or at least a lot of hiding places. So up we went, our pursuers close behind us.

At the top of the incline we saw an elegant archway that looked as though it might lead someplace interesting. And according to Beth's reasoning that meant a lot of tourists who might come to our aid. Too bad she was wrong.

As we hurried through the door, too late we saw we were in another dead end. For there we were, in an octagonal chamber, overlooking the sea. The door by which we had entered was the only way in and out—aside from the small openings high above the jagged rocks on the shore below.

Once again we were trapped, and this time the baby trick couldn't possibly work. Again the three kidnappers closed in on us, the leader waving his sword and his accomplices waving their fists. We backed away from them toward the wall on the far side of the courtyard, but there was no escape!

Suddenly the leader leapt forward and with a long sweeping motion brandished the sword in our direction. But as he did it, he tripped over his robe, lurched over, and by mistake let his sword go flying straight toward us!

Like an arrow flying directly toward its target, the sword flew through the air and hit us! With a small sound of material tearing, the long sword pierced Habiba's robe and kept going. In another second its sharp point had come out on the far side. And there it stayed, its handle sticking in one side and its point coming out on the other. Beth was just starting to wonder why we weren't dead when she realized what had happened: The sword had gone exactly between Leo and her!

But the kidnappers, who still didn't know there were two of us beneath the robes, stood stock still, their silly mouths once again open in shock.

For a second they must have thought they were battling a magic genie, who could be pierced by a sword and still live, for they stood there like statues as we made our escape. Beth did think to remove the sword and throw it out of one of the chamber's windows, down to the rocky shore below.

But as we scrambled through the archway, pushing Teasdale and Daniel in Pamela-Ann's baby carriage, and bumping into one another in our panic, the robe caught on some sharp stone jutting from the archway and the kidnappers finally saw it was just two kids after all—not a genie, not even a Moroccan woman.

So the pursuit started all over again.

We got to the top of the steep part of the road with the villains close on our track. We were completely out of breath, and even Beth, one of the best runners in the world, knew it was just a matter of time before we'd be caught.

Closer and closer they came, when suddenly Teasdale cried out in his bird-like voice, "Don't so worried be! Just hop in with me!"

Praying the baby carriage was strong enough for the three of us plus Daniel, Leo and I leapt in. Since the carriage was at that moment paused at the top of the sloping road, the force of our leap started the carriage rolling down the sharp incline, and at an incredible pace.

"We're going faster than a UFO!" laughed Leo as we rocked, rattled and rolled our way down the hill. We were going so fast we knew there was no way the kidnappers could keep pace with us! What it really was like was a roller coaster going its absolute fastest.

On the run in Essaouira

At the bottom of the hill was an open doorway, and by leaning heavily to one side, we managed to steer the carriage through the door and roll out with lightning speed onto the road beyond it.

"Hi-yo, Silver!" cried Beth as we whizzed down the street, causing Moroccan after Moroccan to leap out of the way. The only one who didn't seem to be enjoying the ride was Teasdale—he'd turned white as milk and looked ready to faint.

Then suddenly our ride was over. A large donkey-cart was in our path, right in the middle of the road, stopped while its owner argued with the donkey who, it seemed, had gone on strike.

There was no way to avoid it: Into the donkey cart we smashed, which ended the journey for Pamela-Ann's baby carriage—but not for us.

The quick stop jolted us right out of the baby carriage and into the air. As gracefully as swallows we flew, over the donkey cart, and into another good-sized pushcart—this one full of very ripe oranges.

There was orange juice everywhere! But that wasn't the worst of it: The force of our arrival caused the orange cart to jerk away from its parked position and roll rather quickly down the busy street. And this time, the cart was too big and heavy to steer by leaning one way or the other—and we were also going too fast to jump off. So on we rolled, gradually losing speed as the road turned slightly uphill as it neared a crossroads where there stood a large fountain, around which rested a number of tourists.

The orange cart rolled in slow motion into the bunch of tourists. The cart was rolling too slowly to really hurt anyone, thank goodness, but still fast enough to knock a few tourists right into the fountain—despite our cries asking them to get out of the way. And who should be among the crowd but Abegonia Leach and her sister Louella.

The cart having been finally stopped by the fountain wall, we hopped off, and Beth was able to hand the enraged owner of the orange cart a hundred dirham bill (around twenty-five dollars) to pay for all the oranges we had squashed. We then ran off giggling down the street.

Our last sight as we turned the corner was of Abegonia Leach clambering out of the fountain, a grim look on her stern face. We couldn't help but wonder if she would try to make the unlucky Moroccan who owned the runaway orange cart write "I will never again be this naughty" fifty times on the blackboard, the way she used to make Beth.

And best of all, the kidnappers were no longer in sight! We had lost them!

Chapter VIII

Ranjom and Rejolution

Our homecoming was stupendous. Our dad and Granny were thrilled, Ed Greyley was absolutely shocked, Habiba started to cry, and even Pamela-Ann seemed slightly pleased—once she got over the loss of her baby carriage. Lord Hodgson said we were "jolly brave children" and Lady Hodgson was simply speechless with wonder.

Our dad took the three of us to the fanciest hotel in Marrakech for dinner and our granny didn't even tell us to clean our fingernails and comb our hair!

Over dinner, our dad told us some bad news: A ransom phone call arrived around three hours before we had—and he had paid it!

"How much?" we wanted to know.

"Twenty thousand dollars," replied our dad.

"My!" grinned Teasdale, then added:

> "I hope that ever shall you
> Remember my enormous value!"

And even though this was one of Teasdale's cleverer rhymes, Beth hardly listened; she was wondering what would have happened to Teasdale if our dad hadn't been able to pay. She also began to wonder about a few other things—things she wanted to discuss with Teasdale and Leo only. . . .

* * *

"Listen," said Beth later than night as Teasdale, Leo and Daniel sat on her bed, "I have something important to say."

"Then say it," replied Leo, who was a bit sleepy.

"Our dad's out twenty thousand dollars—and for nothing!" she said.

"I hardly consider myself nothing!" countered Teasdale.

"I didn't mean it *that* way," laughed Beth. "I meant that by the time he'd paid, we'd already rescued you. And that gives me an idea."

"What's your idea?" asked Teasdale and Leo.

"That it's up to us to not only get our dad's money back, but to capture the kidnappers, too!"

"But how?"

"Well, we know a few things already, at least Leo and I do. We already figured out that the person who kidnapped Teasdale knew him, right? So that means it's either the Hodgsons or Jalil or Ed Greyley."

"I still say it could be Moustacha," put in Leo.

"Maybe," considered Beth.

"No," disagreed Teasdale, "I think you're wrong as wrong can be. I didn't recognize the ones who kidnapped me!"

"Of course not," Beth replied, "and that leads me to my second point: Those three men who chased us around Essaouira had to be working for someone else. Remember, our dad said he received a phone call from a disguised voice three hours before our return—*after* we'd rescued Teasdale."

"That's true," said Leo. "But maybe they figured that since Teasdale had already been rescued, they'd hurry up and get the money before our dad found out!"

"They couldn't be sure we hadn't called our dad the second we rescued Teasdale," countered Beth. "Besides, the phones here are so bad you can always tell a long distance call and our dad said the call sounded local. I say the person who made the phone call was in Marrakech and didn't know about Teasdale being rescued! Christopher Columbus!" she added. "Were we stupid! We *should* have called our dad the second we rescued Teasdale!"

"Well we didn't," Leo said. "But I agree with you, Beth: Why don't we try to catch the kidnappers and get the money back! I agree, it has to have been planned by someone we know!"

"But what if it wasn't?" wondered Teasdale.

"Look at it this way," Beth explained. "We have to start somewhere, right? So we start by investigating the people we know, not to mention the kidnappers' old hideout, and anything else we can think of!"

"You've forgotten one thing, sister most dear," said Teasdale. "The important evidence of somebody here!"

"Huh?" said Beth. "What are you talking about?"

"About the things I did hear and see, when they kidnapped me!"

"So tell us!"

Teasdale cleared his throat and began:

"I was strolling down the street with Daniel that day,
And had just stopped to watch some children at play,
A figure in the shadows I thought that I did see,
And before I knew it—"

"Stop!" cried Leo. "Teasdale," he pleaded, "if you tell us the whole thing in rhyme we'll be up for six days! Just tell us in a regular way!"

"But it's more dramatic in rhyme!" argued Teasdale in his stubborn voice.

So we had no choice but to vote on it. Naturally Teasdale lost. Teasdale tried to let us allow Daniel to vote but we refused.

"Well," said Teasdale, "as I started to state, I was watching some children playing marbles, thinking it was a good

thing to write a poem about. In fact, I'd already composed a few lines. The first was—"

"Skip it!" interrupted Leo. "You can tell us later. Just go on with the story!"

"Well," continued Teasdale, "as I was watching I halfway observed somebody in the shadows. So I went over to look. And the second I did, someone grabbed me, put a hand over my mouth and threw me in a bag. I wriggled like crazy but I just couldn't get free. Then they carried me to that room where they tied me up and left me on the floor. Luckily they didn't notice what skinny wrists I have so I was able to get my left hand free. I quickly put my pen where you could find it—"

"What made you think we'd find it?" wondered Beth.

"I know what good investigators you are," explained Teasdale, "so I figured if anyone could find me, it would have to be you. Anyway, then the kidnappers received a phone call—and from someone speaking French."

"How'd you know the person was speaking French?" Leo demanded.

"Because they answered in French. I even heard the kidnapper on the phone—it was Saïd, I think—say it was a good thing he spoke French, not English, otherwise I'd understand what they were saying!"

"But you speak French!" said Beth.

"*Bien sûr!*" replied Teasdale. (That means "of course.") "But the kidnappers didn't know that!"

"So what else did they say?" demanded Beth.

"I could only hear one side of the conversation," Teasdale explained. "But I heard him say, 'Yes, Marrakech is too dangerous to keep him in. Which hideout shall we take him to?'"

"Aha!" exclaimed Beth. "This means they have more than one hideout! Did you hear anything else?"

"One more thing. He then said he was too tired to drive

61

that far, all the way to someplace beginning with the letter 'Z,' and couldn't they just take me to Essaouira. That's when I wrote the letter 'S.' I thought Essaouira began with an 'S.' So that's where they took me. And the rest you know."

"Good!" said Beth. "We know enough to start investigating. Tomorrow we begin! Are we all resolved to do this?"

"Roger!" agreed Leo happily.

"You bet!" Teasdale announced, and then said:

> "To catch that kidnapping rat,
> I'd even go and eat my hat!"

Chapter IX

A New Conspirator

We started investigating like crazy!

Our first investigatory visit was to Arielle Dorléac, the little French girl who had been kidnapped at the airport the day of our arrival. Like Teasdale, she had been ransomed for twenty thousand American dollars and, rumor had it, was still in a state of shock over what had happened to her.

We found Arielle's house in the new part of town and knocked on the door. With Teasdale as spokesperson we told the maid who answered that we were schoolmates of Arielle's and were there on a visit.

Arielle was sitting quietly in her room when we arrived, gazing out the window, a book in her hand and a black cat purring on her lap. The morning sun glimmered in her hair. She looked very pretty and very sad.

She gasped with surprise when she saw us, but Teasdale quickly assured her we meant no harm. He then told her all that had happened to him and the two launched into a long discussion of their experiences while being kidnapped. Teasdale told us later that Arielle said it had been very good for her to have had the chance to talk with Teasdale, that talking about her horrible experience made it easier to live with.

From Arielle we learned two important things. One was that the person behind the kidnappings also spoke English. Arielle, who had lived in Morocco for five years, had learned

Arabic. So when the person in charge had phoned the thugs, at first they spoke French. Then, remembering Arielle was French they switched to Arabic. She overheard one of the thugs saying (in Arabic) that he really should learn English like Fatah—it would come in handy for talking in front of French children and also in speaking with the "Chief," who spoke English so well. We also learned that Arielle had been held captive far from Marrakech, and not in Essaouira. According to Arielle, she hadn't heard the sea and where she was taken was a good deal hotter than Marrakech. So she imagined it must have been somewhere in the southern part of Morocco. Teasdale asked if she'd heard the kidnappers talking about a town beginning with the letter 'Z' and she became all excited. That, apparently, was the one clue she'd been trying to remember since her release.

"Hmmm," considered Beth as we walked home after spending the morning with Arielle, "this means I was right—there just has to be one person behind these kidnappings! And I'd bet my best baseball that Jalil, Greyley, or the Hodgsons is the mastermind!"

"The masterwho?" Leo wanted to know.

"The mastermind," laughed Beth. "The brains behind the operation."

"That makes sense," Leo responded. "But how are we going to find out which one it is? We can't just go up and ask them!"

"Of course not!" Beth giggled. "But we do know something that they don't know we know—thanks to Leo, that is!"

"Namely?"

"That the snake charmer's basket is where they leave their messages! All we have to do is watch it and see who goes there! Sooner or later, one of them is bound to show up!"

"But not if they see us hanging around!" argued Leo.

64

"Right—we'll have to go in disguise!" Beth answered.

"In a baby carriage I refuse again to go, until fish walk on land and flowers bloom in snow!" exclaimed Teasdale.

"Forget the baby carriage, silly!" chuckled Beth. "Remember we left it in Essaouira, anyway . . . No, we'll go as beggars!"

"Beggars?" wondered Leo.

"Just look around you," Beth explained. "What do you see a lot of in Marrakech? Beggars! Those poor people who wander around asking for a bit of money—and more often than not they have their faces completely hidden! It'll make the perfect disguise. No one would even notice us!"

Shortly after lunch, three beggars slowly entered the Djemaa el Fna. One was dressed in a torn sheet we had found in a closet, the second in a grey blanket that tickled and the third in a brightly colored Moroccan tapestry borrowed from the wall of Ed Greyley's house. Beth thought Teasdale looked far too elegant to be a beggar, but he replied he was just an elegant beggar. "To be elegant and poor, is not *that* rare, I'm sure," he remarked.

We stationed ourselves in a large triangle around the snake charmer without being noticed, even Teasdale. A lot of rich-looking tourists passed making comments like "How disgusting! Look at all these beggars!"; but it was mostly poor-looking Moroccans who stopped and gave us money. We couldn't figure this out. But later when we'd asked our granny she said it only went to show that the richer the person was, the less generous. "Though not always," she added quickly. "I myself give to more charities than I can count—and trust you will too when you're older."

At any rate we sat and waited, the hot afternoon sun beating down on our heads and the flies buzzing around our eyes—the only part of our bodies showing at all. On all sides the Djemaa el Fna swirled with life. Thousands of people passed by in the two hours we waited—old men with turbans, veiled women with babies on their backs, young Moroccans in blue jeans, a string of blind men singing to themselves as they walked along feeling their way with canes, and much more besides. And always in the background was the strange music, the drum beats and the horns, the wailed prayers and the beggars' cries, the laughing of children and the low sad sound of old people talking softly to themselves as they passed. It was so wonderful and strange we almost forgot why we were there.

But when things started happening they started with a bang. Turning away from watching a young Moroccan boy walking through the square on his hands, Beth's mouth fell open to see Lord Hodgson walk briskly by—and right up to the snake charmer! Without even pausing to look he dropped a folded piece of paper in the basket and hurried off.

"Aha!" thought Beth. "I knew it was him all along!"

She started to signal her brothers to leave, when out of nowhere Ed Greyley appeared, walking sedately, a big grin on his large square face.

He stopped nonchalantly by the snake charmer, watched for a while as the horrible cobra swayed in the sun, casually dropped a piece of paper in the basket and then walked off in a leisurely way.

"Aha!" thought Beth, "so they're in on it together! I knew it was them all along!"

Beth was once again starting to signal her brothers when she caught sight of Jalil standing on the edge of the crowd surrounding the snake charmer. He looked very nervous glancing around him all the time, putting his hands in his pockets, and then taking them out. He didn't approach the snake charmer, but Beth was sure she saw them exchange glances—and both Teasdale and Leo saw it too.

66

"Aha!" thought Beth when Jalil had wandered off. "He's in on it too! I knew it was him all along!"

She then paused in her thinking and, scratching her eyebrow, murmured to herself: "I didn't know anything all along! It can't be all three! Or can it?"

On the way home we ran into Pamela-Ann. After finding our way through the small winding streets, we had just entered Derb el Hammam when we heard what was by this time an all too-familiar voice:

"*We* don't want any dirty beggars in *our* street," sneered Pamela-Ann. "Get out before I throw this rock at your ugly heads!" she added, picking up a sizable stone.

Since we didn't want Pamela-Ann to know it was really us, we pretended to leave, going around the corner only long enough to take off our robes and stash them in a hole in the wall.

When we returned moments later, Pamela-Ann was there waiting for us.

"You'll never guess what I just did!" she boasted proudly.

"What did you do?" said Beth in a flat voice.

"I frightened away three yucky old beggars with a rock! And boy were they dirty and ugly and mean-looking!"

"With what you did I disagree," Teasdale told her. "I think we should be kind to those less fortunate than we!"

"Oh, dry up with your crummy poetry!" snapped Pamela-Ann and stomped into the house leaving us to console Teasdale who is very sensitive to any criticism of his poetry, even from someone like Pamela-Ann.

That night, after eating one of Habiba's delicious meals, our dad made us play cards with Pamela-Ann for more than an hour. It was not much fun since she cheated nonstop from beginning to end.

Finally she got tired of winning and strutted off to bother Habiba in the kitchen. So at last we were able to hold a meeting in private and discuss our findings.

"We have no choice but to tail all three," announced Beth.

"What do you mean 'tail' them?" Leo wanted to know.

"Follow them, silly," answered Beth. "We'll each take one and follow them wherever they go."

"Even into the bathroom?" wondered Leo.

"No, of course not! You just wait outside when they go in and when they come out you start following them again. Now, here's how it'll be: I'll take Greyley, Teasdale can follow Hodgson, and Leo will go after Jalil. Okay?"

Leo scowled and demanded: "How come you get to decide everything? It's not fair!"

"Because I'm the oldest," replied Beth, "and that's that!"

As she lay in bed that night, Beth heard a sharp rapping at her door, and in walked Granny Bea looking brisk and businesslike. She sat carefully on the corner of Beth's bed, with her posture perfect as always, and eyed Beth severely.

"What's up?" asked Beth sleepily.

"I think you know perfectly well what's up, young lady," Granny Bea replied. "You are putting yourself in unnecessary danger, not only yourself but your brothers as well. I cannot say I approve."

"W-what are you talking about?" said Beth, stalling for time.

"Do not play innocent with me, young lady," sniffed Granny Bea. "I may be as old as Methuselah but I still know when a plot is afoot. I am quite aware of your plans to find the foul villain responsible for the reprehensible crimes which have been rudely terrorizing the innocent children of Marrakech."

Since Granny Bea always uses a lot of big words it took Beth a minute or two to take in what she'd said. When she had, Beth replied: "I don't care if you know! You can't stop us!"

"On the contrary," said Granny Bea, "I am here to offer my assistance!"

"Your what?"

"My assistance," repeated Granny Bea, nodding her stately head so vigorously a strand of silver hair worked its way loose from her bun. "It is more than evident to me that that miserable excuse for a man, that Mister Moustafa, will never catch the kidnappers! In fact, when I think of that incompetent idiot, my blood transforms itself into lava! I feel it is our responsibility as law-abiding citizens to stop this mockery of justice! Although initially distressed when I learned of your plans—and do not ask me how I did—upon further consideration I felt confident it was the only way to trap the mastermind. Not that there is much doubt as to who it is, of course!"

"Who is it?"

"Really!" snorted Granny Bea. "Have you no sense? I am quite sure it must be that untrustworthy Jalil! And I mean, with your assistance, to bring him to justice!"

"Well," considered Beth; "I'm not so sure it's him—"

"He," corrected Granny Bea.

"He," Beth continued, "but I'm sure we could use your help. You aren't going to tell our dad, are you?"

"For the moment, no," replied our granny after a pause. "But on one condition: You must go nowhere and do nothing without informing me! Is that clear?"

"Yup," said Beth. "And with the four of us I bet we find the mastermind in nothing flat!"

"Or so let us hope," said Granny Bea in a quiet voice.

Chapter X

Conflicting Information

So Granny Bea became our general. It was she who coordinated our efforts and told us where to go and when. Even Beth had to admit she was a big help.

Granny Bea approved of the idea of tailing Greyley, Hodgson, and Jalil; she herself would do what she could to tail Lady Hodgson, just in case it was she. She also approved of our idea of disguising ourselves in beggars' outfits, though she was less than thrilled with Teasdale's brightly colored tapestry.

"You look more like a prince than a pauper," she declared. Teasdale finally agreed to abandon the tapestry and wear a blanket like the rest of us if he could bring Daniel along. We accepted this compromise and Teasdale carefully wrapped Daniel up in some white towels Habiba had lent us. Daniel by this time had become quite accomplished in imitating babies. In fact, the little monkey looked really quite babyish. Beth thinks babies aren't exactly beautiful to begin with.

We had to tell Granny Bea about Daniel, except we told her we'd bought him, not that Teasdale had stolen him. To our surprise she rather liked him. She even remarked that he was a lot less monkeylike than some people she could mention.

Our one big problem was explaining what we were doing all day. Even though he really was very nice, Ed Greyley was the nosiest busybody we'd ever met. He always wanted to chat about our day, and of course we weren't about to tell him the truth! Luckily he didn't have the world's longest attention span, so usually Teasdale would start babbling in rhyme and before you could count to ten, Greyley's attention had shifted.

Our dad was no big problem; as long as we showed up for breakfast and dinner and looked happy, he concluded we were having a good time and didn't ask too many questions. He also was busy helping Ed and the Hodgsons get ready for the arrival of Nicholas Andrews, the British banker coming to look over the books.

Our biggest problem was Pamela-Ann. She was harder to shake than a bloodhound. Granny Bea finally came up with the idea of buying ten pounds of Pamela-Ann's favorite kind of cookie, and bringing out some just at the moment we wanted to sneak out. It worked—Pamela-Ann was so busy downing cookies we were able to leave unnoticed.

After three days of investigating, we held a top-secret spy meeting in the courtyard. Ed and our dad were at the Hodgsons and Habiba had taken Pamela-Ann to her favorite bakery so we had the house completely to ourselves.

Granny Bea tapped her pen on the table and the meeting came to order.

"Beth," our granny said, "why don't you begin? And make sure to tell us whom you have been following and precisely what you have learned—now don't dillydally!"

"Well," began Beth, "I've been following Ed Greyley— and I can tell you this: He's an all right kind of guy!"

"And on what do you base this opinion?" Granny Bea wanted to know.

"'Cause he likes sports as much as I do!" explained Beth. "The first thing he does each morning when he leaves the house is to buy an American paper and check the sports figures! Then he'd buy one of the French-language Moroccan papers and read it from cover to cover in a local café. But he'd concentrate the hardest on the pages with sports news on them!"

"If all he does is read sports news all day, then he's not the mastermind, I'd say," commented Teasdale.

"Well, that's not *all* he does," admitted Beth. "That's just the normal part! It's what he does afterward that's the weird part! Christopher Columbus, is it weird!"

"So what is it?" demanded Leo.

"When he finishes his paper Ed scribbles something on a piece of paper, carefully folds it up, then slips it into his pocket. Then he leaves the café."

"But what's on the paper?" Leo wanted to know.

"That's plain as plain to me," Teasdale told him. "He's surely written some poetry!"

"I kind of doubt it," continued Beth, "'cause when he leaves the café he goes straight to the Djemaa el Fna and drops the paper in the snake charmer's basket, wrapped in a five-dirham note!"

"That's worth a dollar," piped Leo after some quick calculations.

"Anyway," Beth went on, "Greyley would either return home to talk with our dad, or he'd potter with his computer, or meet with Lord Hodgeson, or maybe a client. But after lunch, he'd go to this dirty old restaurant and sit at the farthest table and—"

"What I'd like to know is to which restaurant did he go?" inquired Teasdale.

"It's called the Atlas Café," said Beth. "Why do you want to know?"

"I'll tell you . . . in a minute or two," Teasdale replied.

"So," continued Beth, "there in the Atlas Café, Greyley would be joined by a young Arab man."

"Jalil, no doubt!" snorted our granny.

"Nope, Granny, someone else," corrected Beth. "Anyway, Greyley and the young Arab would talk, and then Greyley would nod and hand the man some money. And I think I saw the young man hand something back, but I'm not sure."

"What do you mean you're not sure?" our granny demanded. "A good investigator is always sure!"

"Well," explained Beth, "a big fat lady passed at just that moment and blocked my view. Anyway, on the way home, Greyley met with a middle-aged Arab man in Western dress on a busy corner, just off the main street in the Guéliz. And they'd chat, look through a newspaper together, and then Greyley would give the man some money. And that," concluded Beth, "is what Greyley did. Sometimes he'd return home looking pleased, sometimes he'd look upset and sometimes he did these things in a different order—but he always did all of them!"

"Merciful heavens!" sniffed Granny Bea. "Greyley seems to be giving money away like water! He sounds as trustworthy as a flea! I, for one, would not invest in such a man's firm! Still, it does not prove he has any connection with the kidnappings—at least none that I can see!"

"And remember he likes sports!" put in Beth. "So he can't be all bad!"

"Time will tell," commented Granny Bea. "Teasdale!" she snapped. "Your turn!"

Teasdale bounced Daniel in his lap and began:

"Daniel and I followed Lord Hodgson all day,
And he's also busy giving money away!"

"Christopher Columbus!" interrupted Beth. "Detectives don't give their reports in rhyme!"

"I do," Teasdale replied. "I'm an iambic investigator!"

"Just make sure you keep it brief," our granny stated. "Now get going!"

"As I was saying," continued Teasdale:

"To the snake charmer Hodgson would go,
And he put money in the basket, you know.
And then he went to the Atlas Café,
And to the young Arab, gave money away!
But when he did these things he looked mad,
And he also looked a bit sad!
Then he went to the Police Headquarters in the Guéliz,
But I couldn't follow him in, so I didn't, if you please."

"Christopher Columbus!" exclaimed Beth. "He sounds as mysterious as Greyley! I mean what is he doing giving all his money away? And why did he visit the police? What's going on around here?"

"Who knows!" said Leo.

"We do not," remarked Granny Bea. "At least not at present. But find out we shall! And we shall bring the criminal to justice!"

But Teasdale refused to believe Lord Hodgson was a criminal, explaining that he'd noticed that while Lord Hodgson had his midmorning tea in a sidewalk café, he read a book of poems by Rupert Brooke, an English poet of the early part of the century and one of Teasdale's favorite writers.

"Anyone who reads Rupert Brooke," announced Teasdale, "can hardly be considered a crook!"

"We will have to wait and see," pronounced Granny Bea. "Now, Leo, your turn. Are you ready?"

"Roger! Ready for blast-off!" Leo replied. "I followed

Jalil, and can you believe it, but he goes to this snake charmer guy too!"

"We already know that from before," interrupted Beth.

"Yeah, but last time he didn't give him money, and this time he did. And Jalil also went to the Atlas Café, and he gave that young guy some money. He even met the guy on the corner Ed Greyley met with and he gave him money too!"

"Christopher Columbus!" exclaimed Beth for the fourth time in less than ten minutes. "It seems like all anybody ever does here is meet with weird people and give them money!"

"Far be it from me to generalize," stated our granny, "but we *are* in an Arab country."

"So?"

"So, in Arab countries, giving people money to either learn something or keep them as an ally is a very normal practice. It is not at all the same as in America where such behavior is usually a sign of illegal activity," clarified Granny Bea.

"Oh, I don't think we'll ever find . . . the one who is the mastermind," commented Teasdale mournfully.

"Nonsense!" snorted our granny. "It is as clear as the nose on your face!"

"What is?" wondered Leo.

"The identity of the mastermind," Granny Bea replied. "You see, I too did my share of observing. And although I was mainly observing Lady Hodgson—and more about her later—I also had the chance to observe young Mr. Jalil on the many occasions he showed up at the house here. And what I saw has me firmly convinced that he and no one else is behind these kidnappings!"

"What did you see?" we wanted to know.

"Patience!" reprimanded our granny. "All things come to those who wait!"

"We're waiting! We're waiting!" groaned Beth. "So tell us!"

"Well," began Granny Bea, "first of all, I observed Jalil sneak into the house when he thought everyone was out except for Habiba and go directly to the room where Ed Greyley keeps his computer. I listened discreetly at the door and heard him fiddling with the computer for a good twenty minutes! Heaven alone knows what nonsense he was attempting with that machine—I for one do not! But I am completely convinced he was up to no good! For why else would he sneak in in such a way? He clearly is up to something!"

"Maybe," said Leo slowly. "Though I don't see what the computer has to do with the kidnappings. Maybe he just wants more practice using the computer. After all, it's a pretty complicated one. I know I had a lot of trouble getting it to work right."

"Well," replied Granny Bea, "you are only a boy. It is natural that you make mistakes on a computer and need time to practice. Jalil is grown and supposedly good with computers. And if he needed practice, I am quite sure all he need do is ask Mr. Greyley. I see no need to sneak about like a common criminal! And besides, why not just go to the main office where the company computers are kept? Why fiddle with Mr. Greyley's home machine? And one more thing, I also saw money pass between Jalil and Habiba, though who was giving and who receiving I cannot say. But I would like to know where Jalil gets the money to be so well-dressed. He dresses better than your father! I must add, however, that I certainly do not suspect Habiba in any way. I am quite sure she has no idea what Jalil is up to! At any rate I am convinced Jalil is up to no good!"

"I'm not so sure," said Leo. "He seems like a nice guy to me! Just because he was messing around with the computer doesn't mean he's involved with the kidnappings! Remember, he's a big computer nut, the way I am! I'm sure he's not the mastermind!"

"*I* would not be too sure!" snorted Granny Bea. "However, we shall pass on to Lady Hodgson."

"What did you learn?" asked Beth.

"For one thing, I learned Lady Hodgson is as dull as dishwater! That spoiled creature never leaves her home except to go shopping or out to lunch or dinner! Though I must say Lord Hodgson strikes me as quite a decent fellow. Anyway, I somehow doubt that Lady Hodgson is our mastermind. She is too busy deciding which dress to wear or which restaurant to dine in to have time to bother with kidnapping innocent children!"

When Granny Bea finished, we all sat and thought for a minute.

"Boy," said Leo, "is this confusing!"

"Not in the slightest," disagreed Granny Bea. "I grant you there are a few loose ends but the finger of guilt points directly at Jalil!"

"No way!" countered Beth. "I say it's Lord Hodgson! He's so polite, but then he gives money to all those people! It has to be him!"

"Oh no, you've reached that conclusion mistakenly," insisted Teasdale. "*Lady* Hodgson seems the mastermind to me! I think she's cold as cold can be!"

"Forget Lady Hodgson, Teasdale," put in Leo. "*I* say it's Ed Greyley! He's so friendly all the time, it reminds me of a science fiction movie I saw, when the friendliest guy in it turned out to be a martian invader in disguise!"

"I somehow doubt Mr. Greyley is the mastermind, much less a martian invader," sniffed our granny. "Though there can be no doubt we all disagree, but we will not for long!"

"What do you mean 'not for long'?" asked Beth.

"I mean do not fret, dear grandchildren. We shall now change tactics! The mastermind cannot stay long hidden from us!"

Or so we thought at the time!

Chapter XI

Pamela-Ann Meets a Magic Gypsy

"Thus far," stated Granny Bea, "We have concentrated on people, and while we have uncovered a wealth of information, we still are at a loss as to what to make of it. Therefore, I propose we change our emphasis. We shall now concentrate on *places* as opposed to people."

"I don't get it," Leo said.

"Then I shall explain further: I shall assign each of you a place to watch—the restaurant, the area near the snake charmer, the police headquarters—places where our suspects go. Perhaps if we know *why* they go there, we'll know who it is we're looking for."

We all agreed that made sense, so Granny Bea assigned us each a place to watch. Beth got the Djemaa el Fna and the snake charmer, Teasdale the Police Headquarters, and Leo the house and the computer room. Our granny assigned herself the restaurant where all three met with the young Arab. We skipped the man on the street, as Granny Bea considered it too difficult to wait all day on a corner.

We continued to see little of our dad during this time; he was still busy working out the contracts for Nicholas Andrews, now due in a few days' time.

Habiba we saw more of, since she prepared and served all our meals. She was as friendly as ever, so friendly it was impossible to imagine she was involved in anything illegal.

Ed Greyley stayed as genial as always; he even tried to teach Teasdale how to play catch in the orange-scented courtyard, but Teasdale hid in the kitchen until Ed put the ball away.

Daniel thrived under Teasdale's care and affection, not to mention all the bananas we fed him. He seemed to be growing before our very eyes and Teasdale was able to teach him two new tricks every day. Daniel's favorites included pretending he was an old man and walking around with a cane, imitating a ballerina, and doing cartwheels across the bed. He also adored playing with the bright silver tea server Lady Hodgson so disliked. In fact, it became his best-loved toy. Daniel had even learned to recognize our footsteps, so he knew how to hide himself when anyone besides Beth, Teasdale, Leo or our granny approached the room. I guess that was how we kept him a secret for so long. Teasdale also gave Daniel a bath every day so his smell wouldn't give him away.

We still had our problems with Pamela-Ann, especially Beth. It seemed Pamela-Ann had decided that she and Beth should be friends—and her way of being friendly was to follow Beth around like a dog, which threatened to put a stop to all our investigations.

"What am I going to do about Pamela-Ann?" wondered Beth on the morning of the day we were going to begin our new tactics. "The trick with the cookies doesn't work anymore. The only time she leaves me alone is when she goes to the bathroom—thank goodness she goes a lot!"

Teasdale, who had been listening to Beth's dilemma, closed his eyes in thought for a moment, and then said:

"To stop that Pam from following you, I have an idea that's bright and new!"

So it was that five minutes later Teasdale ran into Pamela-Ann's room where she was busily nibbling on some cookies she had stolen from our granny's secret supply, and called out:

> "Pamela-Ann, Pamela-Ann—
> Come and help as quick as you can!
> A beggar woman is by the front door;
> The one that you chased away before!"

"I'll teach her a thing or two," muttered Pamela-Ann with her mouth full as she stomped purposefully toward the front door.

"I already told you we don't want any dirty beggars on our street!" whined Pamela-Ann to the heavily draped beggar woman waiting silently on the street. Pamela-Ann then pulled from her pocket a large slingshot, and putting a pebble in the elastic part, began aiming it at the beggar.

"Ooh, ooh—I would not do that, Pamela-Ann," said the beggar in a low mysterious voice even Teasdale hardly recognized.

"How'd you know my name?" gasped Pamela-Ann.

"I am Sabrina, the Magic Gypsy," Beth replied. "And I know all!"

"Sabrina isn't an Arab name," Pamela-Ann announced.

"It isn't?" said Beth. "I mean, it isn't, of course not! I am no Arab, my dear. I come from far away—sunny Spain to be exact—to tell fortunes!"

"Really?" Pamela-Ann inquired, taking a step closer. "Would you tell mine?"

"Yes, my pretty!" replied Beth in a funny voice.

Gazing intently at Pamela-Ann's pudgy palm, Beth began to make low moaning noises and started shaking her head ominously from side to side. She was shaking her head so hard Teasdale started to get nervous Beth's veil would fall off and give the whole trick away. In fact, Teasdale became so nervous he had to go inside and have a glass of orange juice with Habiba, leaving Pamela-Ann alone with the "gypsy."

"What do you see?" demanded Pamela-Ann.

"I see a girl with blonde hair," began Beth. "Tall and athletic."

"Ugh! You must mean that disgusting Beth Smith," Pamela-Ann remarked. "I hate her guts, she's not nice to me!"

"She doesn't like—" began Beth in her normal voice but stopped herself in time. "Yes," she went on in her fake voice, "I see a girl with short blonde hair, one who has two brothers. . . ."

"I don't want to hear about *them!*" whined Pamela-Ann. "I want to hear about *me!*"

"Hold your horses!" Beth responded. "I'm coming to you. Let's see: Ah yes! If you value your life you will stay away from this beautiful and athletic blonde-haired girl they call Beth."

"Why?" Pamela-Ann wanted to know.

"Why?" repeated Beth. "Um—let's see . . . I've got it! Something dreadful is going to happen to her and if you are anywhere near her or her brothers, it might happen to you too! So keep your distance, my little precious, or who knows what might befall!"

"I'll do just that," snickered Pamela-Ann, "and I won't tell Beth a thing about it! And when something bad happens to her, I'll be able to say 'I told you so!' And she'll think I'm so smart she'll be my best friend! Won't that be neat?"

"Yes, very neat," Beth replied. "Now I, Sabrina the Magic Gypsy, must go off to inves— I mean to do my laundry."

"Well, good-bye," said Pamela-Ann. "And I'll remember what you've said. And it better come true—or else!"

"Bye, Pamela-Ann," answered Beth, and walked away as mysteriously as she could down the narrow street . . .

* * *

So we were able to investigate without Pamela-Ann following us around. In fact, from that moment on, Pamela-Ann kept as far away from us as possible. Of course we were all delighted—although later on we felt guilty about it, as you soon shall see . . .

Chapter XII

A Pink Nun, a Stubborn Computer, and an Odd Newspaper

For his trip to the Police Headquarters, Teasdale decided to change disguises. After much deliberation, he resolved that he would be a nun and Daniel an orphan-in-distress. The reason Teasdale would give for lingering around the Police Headquarters would be that he had lost his other orphan-in-distress and was hoping someone would call in information. No one thought very much of this idea except Teasdale, but no matter what we said he refused to change his mind, so finally we had to give in.

Teasdale reported later that everyone at the Police Headquarters was very nice to him. Teasdale imagined they had never seen a nun before. Granny Bea considered that highly unlikely. She thought they had just never seen a nun like Teasdale before since he had draped himself in pink, not black, and wore enormous sunglasses. Even Mr. Moustacha was nice to Teasdale. In fact, he told Teasdale that once he had taken his two children to a fair and had come home with the wrong ones by mistake.

"To anyone this may happen," Mr. Moustacha consoled Teasdale. "Do not let it worry yourself!"

At exactly one o'clock, Mr. Moustacha disappeared into his office after telling his secretary that he did not want to be disturbed. Little did he know that Teasdale the Pink Nun had sneaked into his office when no one was looking and was thus able to overhear every word that Lord Hodgson said when he showed up that afternoon.

"I've got the money here," said Lord Hodgson in an annoyed voice.

"Good!" Mr. Moustacha replied. "Happy it makes me when you me give money!"

"Well, I'm getting bloody tired of it," Lord Hodgson responded. "You know you're not the only one, don't you? I've half a mind to chuck the whole thing and tell everything I know about what you're doing!"

"A good idea that would not be," replied Mr. Moustacha. "Not unless you wish to go to prison and stay there for a while."

"Humph," Lord Hodgson answered, "you have me for the present but not for always! Good day, Monsieur Moustafa!"

"Ah yes, good day to you, too," Mr. Moustacha smiled. "And I see you next week, no?"

Beth kept her "Sabrina the Gypsy" disguise for her afternoon watching the snake charmer in the Djemaa el Fna. It was a broiling hot day and Beth was glad her robes were made out of a light fabric. Seating herself on the ground, Beth adjusted her hood so she could watch the snake charmer without him seeing that her eyes were looking at him.

He was amazingly ugly. The few teeth he had seemed to get longer and yellower each time Beth saw him. He also seemed to spit more each time. Beth had never seen anyone who could spit as far as he did—not that she ever wanted to, of course.

The heat did nothing to still the endless activities that made the Djemaa el Fna the exciting and wonderful place it was. With wandering musicians, acrobats, trained donkeys and fortune-tellers strolling by, it was difficult to keep complete attention focused on the snake charmer—but Beth did.

It was incredible how many people passed by and stopped to talk with him, and people of all kinds—children, beggars, well-dressed Moroccans, Europeans and other tourists too. Sometimes the snake charmer would give the people who stopped money, and sometimes they would give money to him.

Beth watched the cobra rise and fall in rhythm to the snake charmer's flute and wondered why so many people would stop and talk with him.

Her meditations were interrupted by the conversation of two tourists standing next to her. As one dropped a coin into the cup Beth was holding, the other remarked:

"Blimey! That snake charmer is certainly one ugly fellow! I wouldn't care to run into him in a dark alley! Though one can't help but feel a bit sorry for the bloke, sitting out all day in this heat and all!"

"Don't waste your sympathy on him," the other responded. "Believe it or not, Najib there is one of the more important men in Marrakech!"

"What?"

"Najib, that's the snake charmer's name, is actually a powerful figure in local affairs."

"Oh really! Who told you this, anyway?"

"My servant. We happened to pass Najib one day and my servant told me that Najib comes from a rather important family, important more in terms of power than in money or possessions. I can't say how he began, but Najib there is actually a sort of clearinghouse for information about comings and goings around Marrakech. According to my servant, Najib has what amounts to a network of spies that keep him informed about just about everything happening in this town. From some of his spies he buys information, to others he sells information. Apparently he makes quite a bundle. He's also quite feared. And rumor has it he's been involved in more than one illegal operation though the police have never been able to pin anything on him. . . . "

"Hmmm," commented the other tourist, "it takes all kinds, doesn't it? Now where are those shops where I can buy some of those little pointy shoes they all wear here?"

"Some *baboosh?*" replied his companion. "Follow me," he added, and the two disappeared into the crowds.

"So!" thought Beth, "that explains a lot! Or at least a little! I mean at least we know what this guy Najib does. Now all we have to do is find out why Greyley, Hodgson and Jalil go to him!"

Soon after this Ed Greyley showed up and dropped some money in the snake charmer's basket so quickly that Beth almost didn't see it. The snake charmer handed Ed a slip of paper and Ed moved on with a slightly troubled expression. Lord Hodgson showed up later looking cross and a bit tired. He too dropped some money in the basket, but without being given anything in return. Lastly Jalil showed up, and looking extremely uncomfortable, he dropped some money in the basket after which the snake charmer and he exchanged some low words in Arabic which of course Beth didn't understand.

"Christopher Columbus!" thought Beth. "Maybe Granny Bea can figure out what's going on around here! I certainly can't!"

Back in Ed Greyley's house, Leo had quietly sneaked into the room housing the computer and had positioned himself behind some curtains from where he had a good view of the computer.

Ed Greyley was the first to enter. He sat down in front

of the machine and typed in some information. Checking over the readout a few moments later he shook his head and then crinkled up the paper and threw it in the trash with a smile.

"Perfect!" he said to himself and left the room, still smiling.

Shortly after Greyley left, Leo went over to the computer to check it over. It was quite a complex model, more complex than the one Leo had learned on in school. Once again Leo tried out some simple problems, but this time he couldn't get the computer to work at all!

"Boy!" thought Leo. "I must not be as good with computers as I thought I was! Or maybe this machine is broken, or something!"

Leo was about to try again when he heard footsteps outside. There was no time to get to the curtain, so Leo quickly crawled under the desk housing the computer unit.

The door creaked open and soon Leo saw a pair of legs he recognized as Jalil's standing in front of the computer. Jalil said something to himself and started fiddling with the computer without sitting down. He spent quite a while with the machine, mumbling to himself as he worked. He seemed a bit confused, although it was difficult to tell, because when he spoke to himself it was in Arabic. But it seemed he was having as hard a time as Leo with the computer.

Jalil was acting exasperated when voices were suddenly heard outside and two pairs of footsteps approached the door.

Quickly and silently Jalil tiptoed across the room and hid himself behind the curtain.

"Hmmm," Leo considered to himself, "it's a good thing I changed hiding places!"

Our dad and Ed Greyley entered the room and walked over to the computer.

"Here she is," boomed Ed Greyley in his genial voice. "And lordy this machine is one little honey! There's nothing she can't do!"

"Really," responded our dad. "Well, all I need from you now is a printout of your expenditures thus far. The last list you gave me was a bit incomplete. . . . I'd like to have all the facts down pat when Nicholas Andrews shows up. I hear he doesn't let anything slip by him!"

"Is that so?" replied Ed Greyley. "Let me just feed in the necessary information. . . ."

"Good," said our dad a while later. "And now I'd like a printout of your earnings."

"Fine," Ed answered. He then typed a lot of information into the computer and soon the machine had produced a printout.

"Thanks," said our dad as he looked over the sheet. "Now I'd like to ask a little favor, if I may."

"Shoot, pardner," Ed replied. "Always glad to oblige."

"Well," began our dad, "I seem to be having a little disagreement with American Express over some checks I deposited before leaving for Morocco and I'd like to use your computer to go over some of their statements."

"Uh, why sure, James, no problem . . . Though, of course, that kind of calculating's easier on a hand calculator. But, golldarnit, mine's at the office. . . . So let me just get the machine ready for you. . . ."

Ed then punched in some facts or something while our dad waited.

"Ed," said our dad, "I may not be a computer whiz, but how come you had to feed in information just so I could use the machine for routine computations?"

"Oh . . ." replied Ed, slightly embarrassed. "Well . . . you see, I invented a way of blocking anyone else from using the machine. That's what I canceled before I printed out the list of expenditures. Then, just now, I typed in a certain code that blocks any possible erasures of vital information. It happened to some friends of the Hodgsons and I didn't want it to happen to me. After all, this ol' machine is linked up to our records at the main office. So after your son was fiddling with the machine I invented a code I can type in that makes any mistaken erasures of information impossible."

"Sounds smart to me," commented our dad and set to work.

A cramped ten minutes later our dad sighed to himself and said, "Darn those American Express people!" and left the room with Ed Greyley. Jalil tiptoed out afterward, leaving Leo alone at last with the computer.

He quickly tried out a few more problems and was delighted to discover he could operate the machine just fine.

"It must have been that code that stopped me before," he said to himself as he left the room. . . .

The Atlas Café was not Granny Bea's idea of elegance. "Less than lovely," she told us afterward. Disguised as a traditionally veiled Moroccan woman Granny Bea had entered the restaurant where the young Arab man met with Greyley and Hodgson.

It was a small restaurant with ten or so little tables crowded into a square room with tiny windows and a dirty tiled floor. The clientele consisted mainly of older Arab men who sat for a long time with their mint tea or coffee, content to just watch the world go by.

Granny Bea found a table by the wall, ordered a glass of steamed milk and pretended to read an Arab newspaper she had bought. As luck would have it, Ed Greyley entered moments later and as the restaurant was crowded sat at our granny's table. He ordered a cup of coffee, nodded briefly in our granny's direction, and pulled a paper from his coat pocket and started to read.

From behind her veil Granny Bea watched Ed Greyley with an eagle eye. And what she saw struck her as definitely worth seeing. For what Ed Greyley was reading was not an ordinary newspaper—not at all.

"What was it?" asked Beth that night as Granny Bea was telling us her adventures.

"A racing paper," said our granny with no small disgust.

"What's that?" we wondered.

"A racing paper is quite simply a journal devoted to racing—in this case, horse racing. In other words, our good host Mr. Greyley bets on the horses."

"So," said Beth, "what's wrong with that? It's not illegal or anything, is it?"

"Unfortunately not," Granny Bea replied. "It does, though, confirm my opinion of Ed Greyley as a man who is careless with his money. However, it has nothing to do with the kidnappings, at least as far as I can see."

"So how does this help us?" Leo demanded.

"I'd say it explains what Ed Greyley does when he meets with the man on the corner—he places bets! It also could explain why he visits the snake charmer. Perhaps he is receiving tips on horses on which to bet. And then when he wins, perhaps he gives the snake charmer a bit as repayment."

"That makes sense," considered Beth. "After all, that tourist I overheard said the snake charmer is a clearinghouse for all kinds of information."

Granny Bea also went on to say that she and Ed hadn't been sitting there long when the young Arab man came in and pulling a chair over to the table started a quick intense and almost whispered conversation with Ed Greyley.

"They spoke in Arabic," our granny informed us. "So

unfortunately I could hardly understand a word. But one word that came up time and time again was the word Hodgson. They would say it and laugh! Greyley then left, though without paying the man any money, and was soon replaced by Lord Hodgson. Lord Hodgson, however, paid the man a good sum of money and left without talking at all. I was on my third cup of hot milk by the time that crook Jalil appeared. He and the young Arab discussed both Greyley and Hodgson, and afterward Jalil handed the man an extremely large sum of money. Where he gets that kind of money I cannot possibly imagine. It merely is further evidence that he must be the mastermind!"

It was by that time getting late, so to put our thoughts in order our Granny took pen in hand and summarized our discoveries as follows

I. JALIL: pays money to snake charmer, man in restaurant, and toys around with Ed Greyley's computer. Also spends money he couldn't possibly earn. Also seems to be getting information from Habiba concerning comings and goings in the Greyley house as he manages to show up when everyone is out. Would make good mastermind as he is fluent in Arabic, French and English, and has a good knowledge of Marrakech.

II. HODGSON: bribes Police Chief, man in restaurant, and snake charmer. Is it possible he has to bribe Police Chief simply to do business in Marrakech? Is it possible he and Greyley are just checking up on each other when they meet with man in restaurant? He does not seem the criminal type. Possible mastermind, but unlikely.

III. GREYLEY: also bribes man in restaurant and pays money to the snake charmer. Also bets on horses. Is it possible he pays money to snake charmer to get information on which horses to bet on? Possible mastermind, but unlikely. Too successful with computer company to be involved in illegal schemes. In fact, in its initial period of operation, the Greyley/Hodgson company amassed huge earnings, at least according to printouts supplied to James. But heavy betting might indicate character flaw.

"Well," said Beth, "we sure have a lot of information, but we're not really anywhere closer to finding the identity of the mastermind. And I don't care what you say, I still don't think it's Jalil!"

"Yeah!" agreed Leo. "Everybody knows it's Lord Hodgson!"

"Woe on earth and woe on sea," said Teasdale. "Finding the mastermind is harder than I dreamed it would be!"

"Not in the slightest!" sniffed Granny Bea. "I am just this moment in the midst of perfecting a plan to drive the mastermind into the open! It is quite foolproof!"

"What is it?" we begged.

"I shall tell you the day after tomorrow," Granny Bea informed us, "after I have had the opportunity to give it a bit more thought. I am not sure if your father has mentioned this to you but I shall be out of Marrakech until late tomorrow evening."

"Where are you going?"

"Habiba has invited me to visit relatives of hers in the country. Therefore I propose that tomorrow we all take a day off from investigating and do some sight-seeing!"

"That sounds great," said Beth, "though I still wish you'd tell us your plan tonight."

"Tomorrow is time enough," stated Granny Bea. "There

is nothing that can stop an idea whose time has come!"

But little did we then know what *really* was going to happen the next day!

Chapter XIII

An Extremely Unpleasant Surprise

By afternoon we were on a bus chugging through the mountains south of Marrakech and beginning to wonder if we had done the right thing.

"Granny Bea'll kill us when she finds out!" exclaimed Beth.

"If we survive this bus ride!" Leo responded. "This one is worse than last time!"

"Yes, we're cramped as cramped can be," sighed Teasdale. "Buses in Morocco aren't for you and me!"

Teasdale was right. The bus was more crowded than a New York City subway at rush hour, hotter than a microwave oven and noisier than an earthquake. It seemed that every other person on the crowded bus had brought along his radio for the ride and was playing it at full blast. And even though it was broiling hot no one wanted to open the windows. If we'd been eggs we would have been fried after fifteen minutes.

Teasdale sighed and then said,

"This trip is surely no fun—
But it's the least we can do after the wrong we have done!"

"I sure hope you're right," murmured Beth as the bus rattled on. . . .

The day had started out normally. True to her word, Granny Bea went off to spend the day with Habiba. She had left a message for us with our dad. It was short, to the point and read as follows: "Do nothing until my return! Bea."

"What on earth does this mean?" wondered our dad.

"Beats me," said Beth. "Maybe she meant to say, 'Do nothing naughty'?"

"Could be," muttered our dad. "Now listen, kids," he went on, "Ed and I have a lot to do. We can't find a few of the forms we need to get ready for Nicholas Andrews. So I'd appreciate it if you'd keep yourselves busy—and also keep an eye out for Pamela-Ann. After all, you've got each other but she's all alone."

"The reason she's all alone," put in Teasdale, "is 'cause she's the most selfish pig the world has ever known!"

"Enough, Teasdale!" said our dad. He then gave us some money and told us to let him know when we'd decided what we were going to do that day.

After a slight argument, we all agreed we'd explore the Jardin de l'Aguedal, a huge public garden on the southern side of Marrakech. Beth likes looking at flowers and Teasdale thought Daniel would enjoy a day in the country. Leo wasn't wild about the idea but since it was two against one he had to go along with us.

Setting off to say good-bye to our dad, we soon found him with Ed in the computer room and we eavesdropped a moment before entering.

"You've certainly been doing well," our dad was saying. "According to this readout, you've already earned more than you had to borrow from Nicholas Andrews. I wonder if maybe he'll just ask you to pay him back on the spot before negotiating the new loan."

"D-do you think he'd really ask to be paid back?" wondered Ed. "I mean the loan isn't due yet. And anyway, I thought once he saw how well we're doing he'd just add the old loan on to the new, or something like that. . . ."

"We'll see," replied our dad as we made our entrance.

"I think your plan sounds great," our dad said a few minutes later, "except for one thing you seem to have forgotten."

"Namely?"

"Pamela-Ann, of course," our dad said. "Make sure you invite her to come with you!"

"That's right generous of you, pardner," smiled Ed. "But I believe the little niece has some ol' errands of her own she was a-hopin' to do today."

"Well, invite her anyway," our dad said sternly. "I insist."

"Uh, Pamela-Ann," began Beth shortly after we'd talked with our dad, "my brothers and I are, um, going to the Aguedal Gardens and we're wondering if you, um, would like to come with us?"

Indecision flickered over Pamela-Ann's pudgy face. Beth was sure she was about to say yes when Pamela-Ann suddenly blurted out: "No! I don't want to go with you and your smelly brothers! So forget it!" she added and stomped away chuckling to herself.

"What d'ya think she's chuckling about?" Leo wondered.

"About Sabrina the Magic Gypsy," laughed Beth. "That dumb Pam still thinks that something bad's going to happen to us so she won't go anywhere we do!"

"Of all the . . ." muttered Leo as we headed off to the gardens, carrying Daniel in a picnic basket so no one would see him until we got there.

* * *

The Aguedal Gardens were great. We played pirates on the shores of a lovely man-made lake, picked flowers like crazy, spied on Moroccan families on picnics and drenched ourselves in the irrigation system. Daniel had a whirl picking dates, half of which he ate and half of which he threw down on our heads!

It wasn't until around one o'clock that we made our way back to 52 Derb el Hammam.

When we entered the courtyard our dad leapt to his feet, ran toward us like a madman and threw his arms around all of us, all the while crying, "You're safe! You're safe!"

If Beth didn't know our dad a bit better, she'd have sworn he was drunk. Then for a moment Beth thought that Pamela-Ann had told our dad we were all under a gypsy's curse, but that wasn't the kind of thing our dad believed too easily.

"What are you talking about?" Beth asked our dad.

"The note didn't say who it was," he explained mysteriously. "And I couldn't be sure until I saw you all were safe and sound!"

"What note?" asked Leo.

"The note that said: 'We have the child. Pay forty thousand by tomorrow for safe return.'"

It was at this moment we understood: The kidnappers had struck again and Pamela-Ann was their latest victim!

"Ugh!" said Leo. "Imagine having to pay forty thousand for *her!*"

"Leo!" reprimanded our dad. "I never want to hear a re—"

"I know, Dad," sighed Leo. "I'm sorry. I didn't mean to say it. It just kind of slipped out."

We then learned from our dad that Pamela-Ann had left for Guéliz around ten and had been due to return at noon

98

to have lunch with her uncle. By one, when Pamela-Ann hadn't returned or phoned, Ed was starting to get concerned; Pamela-Ann was never one to miss lunch. Just a half hour before our arrival, Ed had discovered the ransom note. He had notified the police and had left word at the Hodgsons to come over the moment they returned home.

"Oh, lordy," Ed was moaning. "We all are gonna have to pay this ransom out of the company's money! I just don't have that kind of money hangin' around!"

"I'm afraid I don't either," our dad told him, "not after ransoming Teasdale . . . But what about Pam's parents? Maybe they could cable you the money!"

"Goll dang it!" cried Ed, "but Pamela-Ann's folks are really in the wilds now. Why, they're even dropped in by helicopter and won't be picked up for another couple of weeks."

"Well," said our dad calmingly, "don't fret. Of course the Hodgsons will be glad to spend company money to save Pamela-Ann!"

"But Nicholas Andrews, he's a-comin' in just a day or two and he'll see all our money'll have been spent ransomin' my little niece! What'll he say?"

"Now, now," our dad replied, "he'll say you did the right thing. I mean, what other choice is there?"

At this point the Hodgsons entered.

"Ed, old chap," said Lord Hodgson, "we received word to come immediately. What is going on?"

"Oh, it's something terrible!" responded Ed. "Pamela-Ann's been kidnapped!"

"But that's impossible!" cried Lady Hodgson.

"It *is* kind of hard to believe," agreed Ed, "but I'm afraid it's true! I have received the ransom note and all! There can be no doubt about it!"

"Oh, Ed," sympathized Lord Hodgson, "how dreadful!

But never doubt Lady Hodgson and I are right behind you, ready to help out no matter what!"

"That's just what I was a-hopin' to hear," began Ed, and went off to speak with the Hodgsons in private.

To pass time our dad was glancing absentmindedly at a map of Morocco, left on the table by Habiba no doubt, who'd probably used it to show our granny where they'd be going that day.

Beth and Leo looked over our dad's shoulder while Teasdale sat dejectedly beneath an orange tree.

"Just think," sighed our dad, "that poor girl could be anywhere on this map."

"For a small country Morocco sure looks pretty big," remarked Beth, beginning to examine the map a bit more carefully. Then something caught her eye.

"Christopher Columbus!" she called out. "Dad!" she went on. "Can I borrow this map for a while?"

"Of course," replied our dad. "But why so excited all of a sudden? You're not planning any more investigating, are you?"

"Us? Investigate? Never in a million years!" laughed Beth as she and her brothers quickly retreated to her room upstairs . . .

"I just figured out something important," announced Beth.

"So what?" said Teasdale. "Don't tell me, 'cause I already know—I figured it out twenty minutes ago!"

"What?"

"We're the cause of all this fuss. Pam wouldn't have been kidnapped if it hadn't been for us!" sighed Teasdale.

"What do you mean?" Leo demanded. "We didn't kidnap her! We wouldn't even *borrow* her!"

Beth looked thoughtful and then said: "I think that's the

100

point Teasdale's making. If we hadn't pulled that Sabrina the Magic Gypsy stunt, Pamela-Ann would have come with us to the gardens and she wouldn't have been kidnapped!"

"Oh, I'm sad as sad can be," moaned Teasdale. "I thought of that plan, so the guilty one is me!"

Teasdale was starting to look so pale that Beth consoled him, saying: "It's all of our faults, Teas. I mean, none of us liked Pam!"

Leo didn't help out any at this moment by crying out: "I can see Teasdale's point! If it hadn't been for what we did I bet they'd never have had the chance to kidnap her. Remember how she used to follow us around!"

Our gloom was interrupted by Teasdale:

"Even though Pamela-Ann stinks in more ways than
    one,
Kidnapping is something that should never be done!
It's uncomfortable and scary and fills you with woe,
And I doubt you need ask how it is I know!
So here then is the next thing to be done by us three:
We're going to rescue Pamela-Ann the same way you
    rescued me!"

"You got it, Teas!" cheered Beth. "And that's what I wanted to tell you. I think I've got an idea where they've taken Pamela-Ann!"

"Where? And how?"

"It's only a guess," Beth explained, "but I think it's a pretty good one. Listen, do you remember when both Teasdale and Arielle were kidnapped? They both remembered the kidnappers talking about another hideout than Essaouira; one that was far from here and began with the letter 'Z'? Well, I looked on the map and as far as I can tell, in the whole of Morocco, there's only one place beginning with a Z and it also happens to be a long way from here!"

"So what is it?"

"It's a town called Zagora right on the edge of the Sahara!"

"Then to Zagora we are bound, where we hope Pamela-Ann is to be found!" pronounced Teasdale.

"But what about our promise to Granny Bea?" demanded Leo. "She'd never forgive us if we broke it!"

"But she's not coming back until late! And if Ed can't raise all the money who knows what could happen to Pam!" argued Beth. "I say we don't have any time to waste. Granny'll understand! Especially if we show up with Pam all safe and sound!"

We left our dad a note so he wouldn't worry too much and grabbing Daniel we dashed to the bus station off the Djemaa el Fna. Soon we were chugging our way through the mountains south of Marrakech, bound for Zagora, Pamela-Ann—and more danger!

Chapter XIV

Up a Tree and in Disguise

It was a long ride.

And it wasn't a very powerful bus. When it went uphill it slowed to a snail's pace and it didn't do much better on the flat stretches. Going downhill it creaked and groaned and shuddered from one side of the narrow road to the other. Beth had the uneasy idea that the brakes weren't especially good but she tried not to think about that too much.

Going over the winding mountain road was the worst part. The road wasn't much wider than the bus and wound around like a snake tying itself in knots. As we tottered around the hairpin curves the valleys below us were so steep it was possible to look straight down from the bus window, thousands of feet below us, to the valley floor where, more than once, Beth saw the burned-out hulk of some bus or truck that hadn't quite made the curve! This didn't exactly inspire a lot of confidence, and we spent a lot of the trip with eyes closed, hoping the driver had his open!

But when our eyes were open we saw a lot of things that were so beautiful I'll always remember them.

We passed through hills the colors of which I had never seen before, strange purples and greens and golds and silvers, colors that changed even as you looked at them. And we saw tiny villages nestled in red cliffs, ancient-looking villages we were sure had stood for centuries. And we passed almost dry riverbeds where local women in brightly colored dresses stood ankle-deep washing clothes. We even saw wild camels galloping drunkenly alongside the road and flocks of goats and sheep with solitary shepherds.

"Well," said Beth, turning away from the window, "I guess this proves one thing."

"That we should have taken a taxi?" suggested Leo.

"No, silly, I'm talking about the kidnappings. . . . No, I'd say that this proves Ed Greyley can't be the mastermind. I mean, it doesn't make any sense to kidnap his own niece," Beth explained. "After all, he has to pay the ransom since he couldn't reach Pam's parents."

"Maybe," considered Leo. "But I say it could still be Ed. He could have just kidnapped Pam to draw attention away from himself. I've heard of criminals doing all kinds of weird things to make people not suspect them."

"Yes, but forty thousand dollars is a lot! After all, they only wanted twenty for Teasdale!"

"That's true," Leo said thoughtfully. "And it sure is bad timing, with that Nicholas Andrews coming to go over the books. He may not be so happy to have company money spent on ransom, no matter what our dad says."

"But Ed will have to pay it back," countered Beth. "And besides, it's not as if they had a choice. I mean no one in their right mind would expect Mr. Moustacha to find a kidnapped child. So the only thing to do around here is to pay up—or hire us!"

"Right!" agreed Teasdale. "And we'll find old Pamela-Ann—if anyone can!"

At five in the afternoon the driver stopped to take a nap and would have slept all night if a passenger hadn't awakened him.

At seven in the evening the bottle of Coca-Cola belonging

104

to the man in the seat in front of us exploded from the heat and the bumpy motion of the bus, totally drenching the man sitting to his left. They had such an enormous argument the bus driver had to stop the bus and yell at them for fifteen minutes to make them stop fighting.

At nine in the evening one of the chickens belonging to the lady in the seat behind us laid an egg, which its owner proudly gave to Beth as a present. Beth wasn't sure what to do with it so she gave it to Leo. Leo didn't know what to do with it either so he gave it to Teasdale. When the bus stopped for ten minutes in a funny little town called Ouar-zazat he fed it to a hungry dog who seemed very pleased.

At seven the next morning the bus rolled into Zagora, a small flat town with one long main street lined with one- and two-story buildings and a mosque or two but not much else. The desert stretched off to the right and tall greenish hills towered on the left.

Beth looked around her in disgust and said, "Ugh! What a dump!"

Leo looked around him, shook his head, and remarked, "Fifteen hours of torture and all we get is this?"

"It's better than the bus," replied Beth uncertainly. "At least I think so."

The hot Saharan wind blew a gale of sand into Beth's eyes as she stood there wondering how on earth we'd be able to find Pamela-Ann in that dusty old town.

"Listen, boys," she began, "before we start investigating let's have a bite to eat. I'm famished!"

"I'm quite hungry too," agreed Teasdale. "So eating's what I'd like to do!"

After a leisurely breakfast we began exploring Zagora. An hour or two of investigation turned up nothing except a banana tree Daniel climbed and refused to come down from.

We had no choice but to stand under the tree and shout

105

for Daniel to come down, but Daniel's only response was to throw banana peels down on our heads! Not until it was too late did we notice that a crowd of Moroccans had gathered behind us to watch us screaming at the tree—or so they must have imagined it.

"Christopher Columbus!" remarked Beth. "Look at all those people!"

Teasdale and Leo turned to look—when all of a sudden Teasdale began looking as though he were seasick.

"What's wrong?" demanded Beth.

"It's they!" he said. "The kidnappers!"

We looked more closely at the crowd and saw Teasdale was right.

"Sssh!" commanded Beth. "Act casual. When they leave we'll follow them!"

"Uh, Beth," Leo said, "I think it's the other way around!"

"What do you mean?" Beth wanted to know.

"I mean it's *them* who are following *us!*"

"Christopher Columbus!" exclaimed Beth. "I never thought of that!"

"Of what?" inquired Teasdale in a trembling voice.

"Instead of *us* capturing *them, they* might capture *us!* C'mon, boys, run for it! Or else we'll all end up being kidnapped!"

We ran. We didn't like leaving Daniel but we had no choice; he was still refusing to climb down the banana tree. If Beth had been by herself she could have outrun the kidnappers easily. But Leo was just too little and Teasdale just not strong enough to run that fast in the blazing Moroccan heat. Even though Beth kept calling out, "Faster! Faster!" the men were steadily gaining on us.

Ahead of us loomed the ugly street, straight as could be and full of strangers who didn't look ready to help a band of runaway children. To our left were a few small buildings

106

with the desert beyond them—certainly no place to hide out there. To our right were a number of streets that led who knew where. And behind us were the kidnappers!

Beth saw the sign *Hotel de Luxe—Spectacles pour les Touristes,* and an arrow pointing to the right, so she shouted to her brothers to turn right and off we ran down a narrow but apparently well-traveled side street.

But it was a dead end.

By the time we realized this the kidnappers had entered the far end.

We were trapped!

"Quick!" cried Leo. "The door!"

Beth looked to her left and saw, on the side of a dull pink building, a door with the words *"Entrée Interdite"* on it. Wondering what *"Entrée Interdite"* meant, we tried the door, found it to be unlocked, and entered, locking it behind us.

"Christopher Columbus!" said Beth. "That was a close one!"

We looked around us. It was Leo who figured out we were in some kind of dressing room, Beth who figured out that the dressing room was part of Hotel de Luxe, and Teasdale who figured out that the dressing room was used by performers in the *Spectacles pour les Touristes.* Teasdale explained that this had nothing to do with eyeglasses but instead consisted of shows with lots of dancing and singing by native Moroccans for tourists.

The dressing room certainly did contain a lot of weird outfits and while Beth and Teasdale were wiping the sweat from their faces with a pink chiffon dress, Leo peeked out the keyhole of the door we had just entered and saw one of the kidnappers waiting on the street.

Trying the other door, he opened it a crack to discover it led right out onto a stage where some musicians were in the middle of some awfully strange-sounding music. And on the far side of the stage were the two other kidnappers, their brown and grey robes standing out from the red velvet curtains.

"They're out there," Leo told his siblings. "And that means we're surrounded."

"Hmmm," Beth mused. "What about the audience? Do you think they'd help us if we dashed out and begged for mercy?"

"I wouldn't bet on it," replied Leo. "It looks like it's a bus-load of Japanese tourists. Who knows if they speak English? They might just think we were part of the act and applaud as the kidnappers dragged us off!"

"That's it!" exclaimed Beth. "Part of the act! We'll be part of the act!"

"Would you mind explaining? I'm finding thinking draining," rhymed Teasdale.

"It's simple," began Beth. "All we have to do is disguise ourselves as part of the act, go out on stage, twirl around a bit or something, and then leave before the kidnappers figure out it was us!"

Teasdale and Leo agreed this was a good idea. Luckily for us we found a program on the floor telling the order of the acts. After the musicians came acrobats (which left out Teasdale); after them came jugglers (which left out all of us); but after them came Moroccan dancers.

"That's the one for us!" beamed Teasdale. "We'll escape with little fuss!"

Teasdale then explained that he'd seen a photograph of Moroccan dancers in one of our dad's guidebooks and he was nearly positive that all they did was prance around the stage in long flowing gowns—and they even wore veils over their faces!

"Perfect!" cheered Beth, and began digging through a

trunk in the corner of the room. Sure enough she found a costume that would do, and taking it in her hands, Beth sat, thinking of the best way to disguise ourselves.

With help from Teasdale our disguise was perfected. Peeking through the stage door Leo announced the jugglers were just leaving the stage. So we quickly donned our disguise and headed for our debut as a Moroccan dancer!

Chapter XV

A Memorable Moroccan Dance Debut

Here's how we did it:

First, Leo placed a piece of red fabric over his face, so only his eyes showed. His head he covered with a flowered bandanna. He then climbed on Beth's shoulders, Leo luckily being on the small side and Beth on the strong. Once he was properly balanced Teasdale draped the two in a long piece of orange material that had until only that minute been a window curtain. Once he judged Beth and Leo looked reasonably like one person, Teasdale tucked under the bottom of the window curtain and practiced crawling as Beth walked. It wasn't easy but Teasdale picked it up relatively quickly, at least for someone who's got a D or F grade in gym every year since he started school.

It would have been a lot easier to just appear as three small Moroccan dancers. But we didn't think three midgets would go over very well since Teasdale had told us the dancers were supposed to be somewhat sexy. Not that we looked sexy, but at least we looked like a grown-up, at least sort of.

Peering through a hole in the disguise, Beth saw the jugglers leave the stage and heard the announcer saying something in Arabic. We imagined he must be announcing the next act so we walked out on stage as best we could. It turned out to be a large stage, raised at least four feet above the audience, who were seated at round tables, all drinking Coca-Cola and waving their cameras like crazy.

We saw two of the kidnappers, one on each side of the stage, their hoods still covering their faces. They seemed surprised by our appearance, but we had no way of knowing

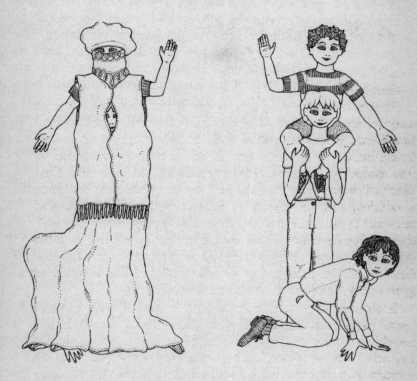

if they suspected something was afoot or just thought we looked surprising—which we certainly did!

The announcer also seemed surprised by our unexpected appearance, but not half as surprised as the other dancer who made her entrance from the far side of the stage. She looked to be in her mid-thirties, was more than slightly plump (fat women being much admired in Morocco), and was dressed in a long red robe with a golden sash around it. She also wore a veil, so at least our costumes matched somewhat.

At this moment the music began, and looking to the other dancer for guidance, Beth did her best to mimic her movements. Fortunately for us, Moroccan dancing begins on the slow side, so Beth had time to get used to balancing Leo on her shoulders, and Teasdale had time to get used to crawling around on the floor at Beth's feet without straying beyond the boundaries of the curtain. More than once Beth stepped on Teasdale's hands, causing him to cry out in pain, but the music was so loud nobody heard except the other dancer who was staring at us in horror.

Finally the first song was done and the other dancer made a low elegant bow. This was where Beth made her first mistake—she bowed too. It started low and elegant until suddenly Beth realized she had leaned a little too far forward—and with Leo's extra weight now swaying forward at a rakish angle, Beth was unable to regain her balance. So with three separate sets of screams we fell flat on our faces. Poor Teasdale ended up on the bottom of the heap and began shrieking at us to get off him, and in a hurry.

Somehow we managed to crawl offstage without separating. But when we got to the exit door there stood one of the kidnappers, his yellow teeth gleaming from the shadows of his grey robe. So we quickly put ourselves in reverse, managed to get back standing up, and reappeared on stage to a thunderous applause. It seemed the audience thought we were a sort off comic number and couldn't understand why the other dancer wasn't as funny as we were. Leo waved his arms to acknowledge their applause and, while the other dancer glared at us with hate in her eyes, the second song began.

This one was a lot faster and we had a hard time keeping pace with our plump competitor. We swayed and tilted like crazy, and more than a few times almost fell. Once we went barreling into the announcer, a small man dressed in a brown robe and a little blue beanie perched on his bald head, and knocked the poor fellow over. But the audience loved it. Beth had never been to Japan but she decided the Japanese must have great senses of humor. They even laughed when one time Leo had to clutch at the stage curtain to keep from falling off and instead ended up pulling the curtain down from the ceiling. They really howled at that one, especially since the curtain ended up falling not on us or on the stunned announcer—silently watching his act being taken over by some weird dancer he'd never even hired—but on the other dancer. She, at the time, was engaged in doing some rapid twirls. So when the curtain fell on her she got herself hopelessly tangled up in it and fell with a thud on her well-padded rear end. The announcer had to go over and liberate her, and when he had, we could tell by the look on her face that this meant war.

It did. During the third dance she did everything she could to either bump into us or trip us or just plain knock us over. But even though Beth had a hard time keeping her balance we were more than a match for our angry friend—since we had two extra sets of arms. When she grabbed Leo's hand in an attempt to pull us off balance Beth was able to reach out with both hands and pinch the dancer's behind in two places. Teasdale meanwhile kept reaching out with his thin arms and tripped her at every possibility. After she had fallen six times she looked at us with awe and gave up the attack.

The third song ended with yet another round of thunderous

applause, flashbulbs flashing and Moroccan coins flying through the air from all sides of the audience, it apparently being a local custom to give money to the dancer during the performance. Beth couldn't help but notice with pride that a lot more money got thrown at us than at our fellow dancer. From his position at Beth's feet Teasdale was able to scoop up the money and stash it in his pockets. And when they got filled up he put the overflow into Beth's socks, which wasn't exactly comfortable. Of course the audience stared open-mouthed to see the coins they'd just thrown disappear like magic into the bottom of Beth's dress. This got them so excited they threw all the more. But the minutes of our stage success were drawing to a close.

The fourth and final song then began. But instead of dancing our fat friend walked to the center of the stage and stood there as though waiting for something. We did the same. And before long two young Moroccan girls appeared, each carrying a large silver platter. On each platter was a silver tea server and around it were a number of glasses. The glasses were filled with water and each glass contained a sprig of peppermint. Also on the tray, placed between each glass and also on top of the tea server, were lighted candles. It was a pretty sight but Beth couldn't imagine why they'd be serving tea to the performers in the middle of a dance.

As Beth watched in mute horror, one of the girls placed her tray on the other dancer's head. As the remaining tray was being placed on Leo's head the fat dancer gave us a nasty grin as if to say, "Bet you can't do this!"

It was at this moment Beth remembered a picture she'd seen in one of our dad's guidebooks. It was a full-page spread showing the various local entertainments tourists could expect to see. Among them was the famed Moroccan tea dance, where the dancer leaves the stage and walks amidst

the audience, all the time balancing a tea tray, complete with glasses of water and burning candles, on her head!

Still grinning at us the other dancer slowly walked down the steps leading from the stage to the audience and began circulating among the cheering customers. Some took her picture, others put money in the sash around her large middle.

"Hmmm," thought Beth, "if that's the only way out, so be it!"

Slowly and carefully she walked down the staircase and entered the audience, heading slowly but surely for the exit.

"Slow down, won't you!" begged Leo. "This tray is real slippery!"

"I'm doing the best I can," answered Beth, "and you're getting heavier by the second!"

"And don't foreget me, the one who writes the rhymes," called out Teasdale, crawling along as best he could at Beth's feet. "My fingers have been stomped on fifty million times!"

As we neared the door disaster struck. For one, the kidnapper guarding the door suddenly figured out for sure it was us and for two, Leo dropped the tray. He claims he dropped it on purpose but Beth doesn't believe him. She thinks it just went sliding off as it had to sooner or later.

A lot of things happened when the tray parted company with Leo's head. First of all we heard the other dancer laugh merrily and then scream. We thought for a second perhaps she had dropped her tray as well but we were wrong. What had happened was that one of the lighted candles had fallen on a paper tablecloth and set it aflame. Screams filled the auditorium and panic ensued. I hope you won't think us unfeeling but we took that moment for our departure aided by a Mr. Yamatori.

A man of fast action, Mr. Yamatori threw the contents of his bottle of Coca-Cola at the fire. It went out in an instant. But to make sure, Mr. Yamatori went to throw his neighbor's Coca-Cola at the smouldering sodden mess that once was a tablecloth. Mr. Yamatori, however, didn't have the world's best aim, nor the best hand control.

When the first blast of Coke hit the fire we had made it to the door, but so had one of the kidnappers. As we tried to pass he reached out a strong arm and held fast. Beth kicked, Leo punched and Teasdale bit, but it was no use; he seemed to have skin of leather. Nothing we did could make him loosen his grip.

Out of the corner of her eye Beth saw the two other kidnappers quickly approaching and at that moment really believed it was all over for us.

But suddenly and seemingly inexplicably the kidnapper let go of us and fell to the floor. Beth was just starting to imagine that perhaps he was prone to fainting the way Teasdale is when she saw what really had happened. Mr. Yamatori's Coke bottle had gone flying out of his hand and had hit the kidnapper hard on the head, knocking him unconscious.

A quick look behind us showed that although the fire was safely extinguished the place was in an uproar. Half of the people angrily demanded their money back for the danger they had gone through and the injury by fire they had so narrowly escaped. Apparently the announcer refused and fighting broke out. Of course we felt guilty for causing all this trouble but then we hadn't done it on purpose. After all, it wasn't our fault that Pamela-Ann had been kidnapped!

At any rate, our guilt was lessened somewhat when we saw two burly Japanese men and one purse-swinging Japanese woman leap furiously on the two conscious kidnappers, presumably thinking them part of the show.

As we wobbled out onto the street, still in our dancer's outfit, our last look as we left our one and only Moroccan

116

dance debut was of a pile of shouting Japanese tourists sitting on the two kidnappers calling them mean names in Japanese!

"This could start a war!" giggled Beth as the three of us stood on the hot dusty street wondering what to do next.

Chapter XVI

The Return of the Yellow Citroën

There we were, standing on the street in a small Moroccan town, disguised as a Moroccan dancer, trying to decide where to go. Suddenly Leo felt someone tugging energetically on his arm. We wheeled around and there stood Mr. Yamatori. We were expecting him to start yelling at us or hitting us when he burst into eloquent French which only Teasdale understood.

"Oh my little sweet," cooed Mr. Yamatori in French, "it is you alone I adore! Ever since I saw you on stage my heart filled with longing! Tell me your name!"

From Beth's feet Teasdale cried out his response, also in French, "My name is Teasdalia!"

Mr. Yamatori looked wonderingly at us. "Will delights never come to an end!" he said. "My little Teasdalia talks with her mouth shut and the voice comes out of her feet! Oh, tell me when we may meet again!"

For want of anything better to say Teasdale responded, "But I don't even know your name!"

"Oh, forgive me, little Teasdalia," our admirer replied. "My name is Kensaku Yamatori and I—"

But we never knew what Kensaku had in mind to say next for at that moment the three kidnappers emerged from the auditorium door.

"Farewell, Kensaku," cried Teasdale, "but we must flee!"

Flee we did with the kidnappers hot on our trail, and once again Mr. Yamatori proved our rescuer. When he observed his beloved Teasdalia being pursued by three robed and hooded strangers Kensaku rose to our defense. As we turned the corner we saw Kensaku's hands and feet go this way and that, after which we heard loud grunts and groans from the kidnappers. Kensaku must have had some talent at karate.

But Kensaku's karate was not enough to delay the kidnappers for more than a minute or two by which time we had clambered out of our disguise and had once again started running.

Once again we also knew how a fox feels in a hunt. We ran and the kidnappers ran after us, and it was about as fair as a fox-hunt, when the men get to ride on big horses and all the fox has are his own little feet. The kidnappers had big long grown-up legs and we were still kids, especially Teasdale and Leo.

It certainly looked hopeless. Although we had a margin of over forty feet, thanks to Kensaku Yamatori, it was only a matter of time before we were caught. Just then we raced by none other than the yellow Citroën 2-CV that Mr. Moustacha had claimed was unfindable. As we charged by, Beth caught a glimpse of something bright and shiny in the car's ignition. It was the key.

"Quick, boys!" called Beth. "Hop in!"

"But none of us knows how to drive!" Leo reminded her.

"There's no time like the present to learn something new," replied Beth, mimicking one of Granny Bea's favorite expressions.

"Though the idea's probably lame, I'm still game," announced Teasdale, adding, "Though with you driving there'll surely be no surviving!"

119

"Tell me about it later!" answered Beth. "Now just hop in and lock those doors!"

The kidnappers were all over the Citroën only seconds after the last door was locked. They beat their fists on the windows and kicked the sides with their yellow slippers as Beth started the engine.

"What do you think you do next?" wondered Beth as the kidnapper on the roof tried punching in the front window.

"You see that stick thing on the floor?" Leo replied. "Well, I've watched when our dad drives and I'm pretty sure you push it around at the same time you do something with your feet."

"Oh," said Beth as one of the kidnappers started pounding on the driver's window with a pointy rock. "Here goes!"

With a burst of power the yellow car came to life and
went careening backwards into the truck parked behind us.
We heard the shattering of glass and loud curses from the
kidnappers as they were thrown off the Citroën. Not having
expected Beth to go backward they had been caught off-
guard.

"I don't think that's how you do it," ventured Leo.

"Of course not!" said Beth. "I only did that to surprise
the kidnappers."

"Oh," replied Leo, without sounding as though he really
believed me. Teasdale didn't have any comment, having
fainted long ago.

Beth tried pushing the gear shift another way and this

time the car shot forward twenty feet and stalled, its un-expectedly short stop causing the kidnapper who had been running behind the car to run straight into it. He fell to the ground with an anguished cry of pain but seconds later was pounding on the rear side window above Teasdale.

"Boy!" said Leo, "if driving a car is this complicated, just imagine what driving a UFO is like!"

"Worry about UFOs later," Beth replied. "Now help me figure out what to do next before that kidnapper breaks the window!"

"Just try the same thing, only more gently," counseled Leo.

Beth tried and sure enough the Citroën glided forward and kept on going. We hooted and hollered with triumph as we proceeded through Zagora, heading south, with the angry kidnappers running after the car, waving their arms and shouting.

The next moment we passed under the banana tree where we'd last seen Daniel. The little monkey saw us passing beneath, threw down a shower of banana skins, and then leapt down on the Citroën's roof. Teasdale de-fainted in time to open the window and pull the monkey into safety.

Our reunion was made even more jolly by the view out the rear window of the three kidnappers skidding all over the road and falling flat on their faces as they encoun-tered the banana peels provided by Daniel.

"You're the smartest monkey of them all," pronounced Teasdale. "Thanks to you the kidnappers have had a big fall!"

Teasdale then looked thoughtful and added, "There's only one thing I'd like to be knowing: And that thing is where are we going?"

"Back to Marrakech, of course," Beth replied noncha-lantly. "Now that I've figured out how to drive it should be easy."

"Except for one little thing," remarked Leo.

"Namely?" Beth wanted to know.

"Namely we're heading south and Marrakech is north of Zagora!"

"Oh," said Beth. "That's no big deal, we'll just turn around."

We had by that time cleared Zagora, which wasn't too hard considering its size, and were passing some low mud huts that bordered the town. They were built in the shadows of some gigantic palm trees, growing alongside the river that provided Zagora's water and ran just south of the huts.

We rolled across the bridge spanning the shallow muddy river, nearly running over two donkeys and an old woman in the process. On the far side of the river was where the Sahara began. Here the road widened a bit, perfect for turning around.

"Here we go!" announced Beth. "Back to Marrakech, home of the brave and land of the free!"

It wasn't Beth's fault that no one told her you're supposed to slow down when turning around sharply and by the time Leo did it was too late.

We took the turn so quickly that the Citroën spun out of control and started heading of its own accord toward a group of men taking a nap on the side of the road.

Seeing that we were about to run over three innocent pedestrians Leo shrieked out, "The brake, Beth, step on the brake!"

"Good idea!" said Beth and pressed what she thought was the brake.

It wasn't. It was the accelerator and before you could count to zero we were almost on top of the sleeping men. Beth tugged madly at the steering wheel, Leo tugged madly at it too, and somehow we managed to avoid the men.

But we didn't avoid the river.

With a thud and a weird squishing sound the Citroën sailed off the road and landed in the middle of the river. The water wasn't deep, thank goodness, but the mud was disgusting. The car slowed to a halt about fifteen feet from the nearest bank and Beth leaned out of the window to survey the damage. It was hard to tell how severely the Citroën had been hurt by its plunge. The mud was up to its door handles.

"Something tells me it's good-bye Citroën and hello feet," sighed Beth.

"Yeah," agreed Leo, "and something tells *me* we'd better get a move on before you-know-who show up!"

I've never understood why Teasdale always seems so much heavier when he's fainted, for our poet brother had fainted the moment the car hit the river. We staggered and groaned under his weight as we abandoned the Citroën and made our way to dry land.

Our welcoming committee on the shore was not Beth's idea of a good time.

From nowhere appeared the three kidnappers. They surrounded us in a second, a kidnapper standing next to each of us, including a de-fainted Teasdale.

"So we meet again!" said the only English-speaking one, Fatah. And sure enough they were the same three we'd escaped in Essaouira.

"Think not to run away," said Fatah in a low voice. "We have each sharp knives in case you so decide."

At that moment we each felt a sharp prick in our sides from knives held discreetly under the kidnappers' grimy robes.

"If you'd only let us free I'd write you some poetry!" cried Teasdale desperately.

"The next one who shall talk shall feel a big hole in his side where a knife has gone in!" said Fatah quietly.

Leo gulped, Teasdale looked faint and Beth waited to hear what would happen next.

"Follow!" ordered Fatah as we set off, back toward Zagora.

124

It was by that time midafternoon and as we walked in silence with our captors the heat was terrible. We all wondered where we were being led.

After leaving Zagora's main street we followed the kidnappers down dark alleys and dirty streets until at last we arrived at a small door on an especially filthy side street. After unlocking it the kidnappers ushered us into a small apartment.

We were then brought into a small room, clearly some sort of storeroom. It had a musty disused smell and contained nothing but a rusty set of springs for a mattress and a rough wooden stool which was simply a ratty old cushion nailed onto a hollow wooden box. There weren't even any windows.

"It is here you stay," our hooded captor told us.

We were shoved toward the far side of the room and the door was slammed and locked behind us. But seconds later it was opened again and Fatah appeared.

"We have here another child," he told us, "so we put you all together so we know where you are!"

"Here comes Pamela-Ann!" muttered Beth. "Even though we came all this way to rescue her she's still the last person I feel like seeing!"

"Yeah!" agreed Leo. "We have enough problems without *her!*"

"Here is your little friend!" announced the kidnapper. Opening the door a crack, he shoved in the reason for our dangerous trek to Zagora.

But our mouths dropped open as we examined our new companion.

"Christopher Columbus!" gasped Beth. "You're not Pamela-Ann! Who in blazes are you?"

"My name is Manheim Schinkengruber!"

Chapter XVII

Under the Eyes of a Most Evil Guard

Manheim Schinkengruber was a healthy-looking boy around ten years old. While we all were in various stages of sloppiness, not to mention being still wet and muddy from our dip in the river, Manheim was the picture of spotlessness.

Looking with disgust in our direction, Manheim announced in a loud voice: "You are very dirty children. I do not wish to know you."

"Christopher Columbus!" exclaimed Beth. "We travel hundreds of miles and risk our necks to rescue you and this is all the thanks we get!"

"As I recall," said Manheim, "you came here hoping to rescue someone named Pamela. You did not come to rescue me. You must be very stupid children to travel so far to rescue someone you do not even know."

"Of all the——" began Leo angrily.

"Please do not talk anymore to me," Manheim said. "And I will not talk to you. In Germany, where I come from, one does not talk to people one doesn't know, especially people as messy as yourselves!"

"I don't care if you talk with us or not," Beth told Manheim, "but we're here to rescue you anyway! So there!"

"I do not wish to be rescued by ill-dressed people I've

never even met," replied Manheim. "And doubtless my father will by this time have sent the limousine to collect me!"

"I don't think he's even sent a postcard, much less a limousine," argued Beth. "There's been a mix-up: The ransom note must have been delivered to the wrong place. Your father probably doesn't even know you've been kidnapped!"

"But he'll know something amiss has happened to me even though I refused to write him a letter, as the kidnappers told me to," Manheim informed us. "You see, I was due in our hotel in Marrakech at four fourteen yesterday afternoon. When I did not arrive, I am sure he informed the police. I am never late."

"We happen to know the Chief of Police," replied Beth, "and if you're expecting him to find you, you'll be here a good long time!"

"I do not believe you," Manheim snapped. "In Germany the police know how to do their jobs."

"Oh, but Manheim, don't you see," interjected Teasdale. "Germany's not where we happen to be!"

Our argument was interrupted by the reappearance of the three kidnappers. One held a large basket and the other two ropes.

"We have something to tell you—" began Fatah.

"And *I* have something to tell *you!*" Manheim burst out. *"I* am Manheim F. Schinkengruber and *I* am an important German, much more important than those other three—" he was saying when one of the kidnappers slapped him across the face. And even though this was something Beth had wanted to do herself, she still didn't like seeing it done.

"Hush!" commanded Fatah. "You will listen while you are tied up!"

As Fatah watched, the other two kidnappers, Achmed and Saïd, tied us up. Beth was tied back-to-back with Manheim and then the two of them were tied to the corner of the box springs. Teasdale, who had just that minute fainted, was tied to the box springs in a lying-down position, and Leo was tied last of all to the stool. He had squirmed around the most during the tying up and one of the kidnappers slapped him.

"Coward!" called out Beth when Leo had been hit. "Only a coward hits a little kid!"

But all Beth got for her statement was a smack from another of the kidnappers. And can you believe it, but they even tied up Daniel—next to Teasdale on the box springs.

While we were being tied up Fatah had continued speaking: "We must go do something. But we return soon. It seems you have a talent for escaping," he said mockingly. "So in case these ropes don't hold you, I doubt you would care to pass the one I leave to guard you. Now we must go off but back we shall come soon. Now I show you your guard."

And saying this Fatah directed the other two out of the room and himself stood by the door. He then placed the basket he'd been holding on the floor.

"He will attack anything that moves," he told us as with his foot he knocked over the basket and quickly left the room, shutting and locking the door behind him.

"What do you think he was talking about?" Beth wondered aloud when a gasp from Leo turned her attention back to the basket.

For from out of the basket, coil after shiny coil, appeared a cobra. He recoiled himself right by the door in tight loops, all except his upper body that is. That part stayed upright, swaying back and forth, his evil tongue darting in and out in small rapid motions. He seemed to be watching us intently, especially Daniel.

He was the ugliest thing I've ever seen.

Beth uttered a shriek and Teasdale, who had momentarily returned to consciousness, took a look at the cobra and fainted on the spot. As for Leo, all the color had drained from his face and he was covered with sweat. He was so scared you could smell it.

"You are cowardly children," Manheim informed us. "And stupid ones too. I am sure this snake doesn't even have fangs, so being frightened is foolish."

"Oh yeah?" said Beth.

"Of course he doesn't," Manheim explained. "In Germany it is against the law to let poisonous snakes go running about loose. *Everybody* knows that!"

"Christopher Columbus!" groaned Beth. "It's also against the law to go around kidnapping children, in case you forgot. And anyway, we're not in Germany!"

"I wish I were," replied Manheim.

"You're not the only one!" put in Leo.

"Stop arguing!" interrupted Beth in an urgent voice. "I just thought of something!"

"What?" we all demanded.

"It's not good," warned Beth, "but here goes: Listen, I bet I know why the kidnappers left. They probably had to phone the mastermind, because of the trouble they're having!"

"What trouble?"

"If they kidnapped Manheim here but by mistake delivered the ransom note to Ed Greyley, why, when Pamela-Ann returns from wherever she went—"

"A long visit to the bakery, no doubt," suggested Leo.

"Anyway," continued Beth, "when Pam gets back, Ed won't pay the ransom. Why should he? He'll find out Pam was never kidnapped and figure it was all one big hoax."

129

"So if Ed won't pay," Leo suggested, "then the kidnappers'll send our dad a ransom note, and it'll be for a lot—considering they have all three of us!"

"That's the other problem," replied Beth. "Our dad's already paid out twenty thousand for Teasdale. It would take him a long time to raise the other money. He'd have to go back home and sell something!"

"So it'll just take a little time," Leo answered.

"Maybe too much time!" replied Beth ominously. "What happens if the kidnappers get sick of waiting? What if they don't believe our dad needs time to raise the money? What would happen to us?"

"In Germany—" began Manheim.

"Forget Germany!" Beth interrupted. "Those kidnappers are crazy! They might get nervous waiting and think the police were on their trail. I mean, they'd figure if *we* could find where they were, then so could the police!"

"You're right!" said Leo.

"And," Beth went on, as she watched the cobra still watching us, "I wouldn't be surprised if . . . if . . . if . . ."

"If they came back and killed us!" gasped Leo.

"Mein Gott!" said Manheim. "Perhaps you are correct even though you are not clean! We must get out of here!"

"And quickly too!" Beth added. "I bet when they finish speaking with the mastermind the next thing they'll do is fish the Citroën out of the river, then come back to get us! And you know what that means!"

"It means we better get out of this place!" cried Leo.

"But how?" wondered Beth. "If we move at all that *thing* over there attacks! We can't even get our hands free to hit him with something!"

"Maybe you can't but I can," said Leo in a small voice.

"What do you mean?" Beth asked.

"I mean that when the kidnappers were tying me up I

130

wriggled around so much that when they tied my wrists together the knots were a bit loose. I saw someone do that once in a movie, *Jailed on Jupiter* was the name of it, so I did it too. And I just this moment got both hands loose!"

"Good for you, Leo!" cheered Beth. "I knew you could do it!"

"But what next?" demanded Manheim. He always seemed to ask the toughest questions. Maybe when he grows up he'll be a teacher.

"I'm—I'm not sure . . ." Leo replied.

"Can you get your legs free without the cobra seeing you?" asked Beth.

"I—I think so," answered Leo, and slowly lowered his free hands to his ankles and fiddled around for what seemed like a year.

"Done!" he finally said.

"Great!" cheered Beth.

"Now what?" demanded Manheim.

We all thought, even Teasdale who had by then de-fainted. But no one could figure anything out until at last Leo said in a tiny voice:

"I know what I have to do. And I'm going to do it, at least I hope so. And if I don't make it, then I'll—I'll—I guess I'll get a chance to see our mom or something. . . ."

"Leo!" began Beth and started to cry. Teasdale was crying too. Even Daniel was whimpering sadly. As a matter of fact, the only dry eyes in the room belonged to Manheim and the cobra. Leo's eyes were red as for the first time he looked long and hard at the cobra.

The cobra seemed to be staring back at Leo. For a moment Beth was convinced Leo would faint. But no, he bowed his head for a moment, looked as though he might be praying, and moved into action.

Beth had never in her life seen anyone move so quickly.

Leo leapt to his feet and took the stool in his hands. He moved rapidly toward the cobra at the same time the cobra was moving toward him, its awful tongue sticking way out and its body arched as if to strike.

And strike it did—but Leo struck first! With a crash the stool came thundering down on top of the cobra, trapping it in the hollow section under the cushion, where we could hear it hissing and writhing about.

Leo burst into tears from his position atop the stool. Being scared can do strange things to a person: Leo usually never cries.

"Leo!" cried Beth. "I'm so proud of you!"

And Teasdale was even recovered enough from his faint to make up a little rhyme:

"I sing you the praises of brave Leo Smith,
There's no greater hero in legend or myth!
Although of snakes he is truly afraid,
He conquered a cobra without any aid!
All that he used were a stool and his wits,
And I'm so proud I could hug him to bits!"

Manheim, however, was not impressed.

"That was really *dumb!*" he announced, and then explained that even though Leo had the snake trapped under the stool if he got off the stool to untie us, the snake could get free and we'd be back where we started.

"Maybe Leo could move the stool across the room without picking it up 'til he got where we are and then untie us," suggested Beth. But when Leo tried, the floor proved too rough and uneven.

Once again we were plunged into thought and once again there seemed to be no ready answer. And as time went by we all prayed the kidnappers wouldn't return soon!

We were just about to give up hope when Teasdale noticed that Daniel had been able to gnaw through the ropes binding his wrists. Teasdale thought for a second and then said:

"C'mon little monkey, c'mon little Dan,
If you can't do it, nobody can!
Untie your feet and when you get them free,
Come over and do the same thing to me!"

"What a waste of time!" mocked Manheim. "You're a dreamer if you think a filthy monkey can understand you!"

But to everybody's surprise except Teasdale's, Daniel did understand, and before long we were untied and free. We put the box springs on top of the stool and then broke the door open. Here Manheim actually came in handy—he was a very strong boy.

It was by now early evening and the dark blue skies beyond the town were starting to twinkle with stars.

"What now?" wondered Leo.

"It is clear to me," responded Manheim. "We go to the local police and turn ourselves in."

"But what if the police are in league with the kidnappers?" demanded Beth. "That *could* be why they chose Zagora for a hideout!"

"Impossible!" disagreed Manheim. "In Germany the police would never be in league with kidnappers!"

"Christopher Columbus!" groaned an exasperated Beth. "We're not in—"

"Forget this talk of Germany!" counseled Teasdale. "Up the street I see a certain three!"

So with Manheim complaining bitterly, the four of us, plus Daniel, turned tail and ran down a dark street in a strange town with the kidnappers once again on our trail!

Chapter XVIII

On a Magic Carpet Ride

"Quick!" shouted Beth. "Turn right!"

Following Beth's direction, we all darted into an open doorway—even Manheim. The doorway led to a side street lined with shops, and though it was evening they all were open.

"Listen!" barked Beth. "We can't outrun them. We've got to hide!"

"I do not hide!" announced Manheim. "I face my enemies like a—"

"Tell us later!" interrupted Beth. "Now c'mon!"

The second the kidnappers turned the corner onto the street where we'd been standing, we disappeared into a cavernous rug store.

Luck seemed to be with us. The owner was busy deliberating with a customer and didn't notice us come in. We ran to the back of the shop and found an enormous storeroom filled with large rolled-up rugs.

"Hurry up!" commanded Beth. "Into the carpets!"

"*Into* the carpets?" wondered Leo. "Are you nuts?"

"Not at all," Beth whispered in an urgent voice. "It's the perfect hiding place! Look, they're all rolled up, but not too tightly. There's a hollow place inside each one large enough for us to hide in without being suffocated! Hurry!"

Beth and Leo squirmed into the nearest carpets but leave it to Teasdale to spend a good three minutes selecting the carpet he considered the prettiest. As for Manheim, at first he refused to hide in the carpets at all!

"They look much too dirty," he informed us. "I might muss my clothing!"

But the arrival of the kidnappers at the front of the shop changed his mind.

We had just hidden ourselves when we heard footsteps entering the room and the loud angry voices of the kidnappers. We heard them look behind a few rugs and then leave.

Just as Beth was about to announce the "All clear" and start to crawl out, the footsteps returned and the next thing we knew we felt ourselves being tilted at odd angles, and we were carted off. Beth prayed that the people doing the carting were rug buyers and not the kidnappers. But since they didn't speak we had no way of knowing.

I don't think being a carpet must be especially fun; we were knocked around like crazy. You'd need a calculator to count the number of times we were dropped, kicked, punched, and rolled along the rocky alleys. Luckily the carpets were relatively thick so it was a lot less painful than it might have been.

To make sure we were all still together Beth gave a brief birdlike whistle, one of our secret signals. She breathed a sigh of relief to hear Leo's response and then a moment later Teasdale's. Even Manheim figured out we were signaling to one another and gave a little whistle.

Suddenly Beth had the impression her rug was flying up high, then as suddenly all was still. Straining her ears against the side of the rug that surrounded her, Beth could make out a babel of voices, all screaming and shouting, none making any sense. She was about to crawl out and hope there were no kidnappers around when she heard, from far below her, a sound she couldn't quite identify. At first it sounded like waves on the beach and then like a giant cat purring. It wasn't until Beth felt herself moving fast, with the cold night air whistling through the open ends of her carpet that she began to guess what had happened.

Inching herself forward slowly and carefully, Beth was at last able to peek out of the end of her carpet—and what she saw took her breath away. If she had been Teasdale she would have fainted.

Our carpets were part of a huge stack loosely tied to the top of a bus. The bus was speeding down dark roads, through the mysterious desert night, to who knew where, and with us on the top!

There is only one thing worse than riding *in* a Moroccan bus and that's riding on *top* of a Moroccan bus! The wind roared through our rugs and we were bounced around like basketballs. It was awful to notice how loosely we were tied down to the top of the bus. There was just a small railing around us, a few carelessly tied pieces of rope, and that was all! A good-sized bump in the road or a sudden stop and Beth feared the rugs would go flying, and perhaps into one of those deep ravines we had passed on the trip down to Zagora!

Peering to her right, Beth made out five or six other rugs and she wondered which contained her brothers and Manheim. It was impossible to check as the bus was in motion, but soon Beth saw a head poke out from the rug nearest hers.

"This must be what riding in a UFO feels like!" said Leo bravely.

"Where's Teasdale?" Beth asked.

A third head appeared, along with a small monkey-sized one.

"Riding on top of a bus just isn't for us!" sighed Teasdale.

136

Manheim was the last to appear.

"This is not the way I would wish to be rescued," he announced.

We thought briefly of all trying to crawl into the same rug, but gave up the idea as too risky, so we stayed where we were and chatted as best we could in the roaring wind and the darkness.

After a time Teasdale announced he was feeling faint and was going to crawl into the middle of his rug with Daniel in case he actually fainted. Manheim too retreated into his rug so Leo and I were left alone.

We talked awhile about how exciting it all was, then gave up. The wind was too strong and we were getting too cold.

"See you in the morning!" said Leo and disappeared into his rug.

Beth kept her head out a bit longer, liking the feel of the wind in her short hair and the sight of the strange shadows cast by the headlights of the ancient bus as it chugged up steep mountain passes and then rolled quickly down the inclines. Occasionally she could spot twinkling lights in the distance, lights from windows in the small mountain villages we had passed on the trip down. Tears came to Beth's eyes as she thought of people safe at home and warm and comfortable.

Taking one last look, Beth too crawled into her rug and soon fell asleep. . . .

The next thing we knew we were being lugged down a noisy street and before long were dumped rudely on the ground somewhere. We heard loud voices, then footsteps, and finally silence.

Next we heard a man's voice humming—and before she

knew quite what was happening Beth's rug was unrolled so suddenly she went flying out the end and rolled ten feet across a tiled floor and into a fountain.

"Quoi?" said the voice and Beth looked up to see a young man standing with his mouth open in shock and his eyes wide in horror and surprise.

"Hi!" said Beth as she clambered out of the fountain and to her feet. She was in a small courtyard, standing by a blue-and-white tiled fountain, gazing into the hazel eyes of a stunned Frenchman.

"Qu'est-ce que—" he began.

But Beth interrupted, saying: "Sorry—but I don't speak French. Let me unwrap Teasdale!"

There were three other rugs on the floor of the courtyard. The first one Beth tried contained Leo, who though filthy and sleepy was none the worse for wear.

"Bonjour—" began the Frenchman, who had by this time lit a cigarette and was puffing frantically on it.

"Nope," Beth told him, "that's not Teasdale, that's Leo, and he can't speak French either!"

The next rug contained Manheim, who was in a foul temper. *"Gott im Himmel!"* he said, and then added, *"Shreck!"*

"Oui?" responded the Frenchman and sat down on a small cushion in a tiny alcove overlooking the courtyard. He was staring at us though we were martians and his mouth fell open even further when Beth and Leo went to the final rug and unwrapped Teasdale and Daniel.

Daniel was fine, but Teasdale rolled out in a dead faint which hardly surprised us but seemed to horrify the Frenchman. Perhaps he thought Teasdale was dead. But Leo and I just picked up Teasdale and dipped his head in the fountain and before we knew it he was alert and de-fainted.

"Talk to him!" said Beth to Teasdale, pointing at the young Frenchman, who had just poured himself a glass of wine and was puffing on his second cigarette.

Teasdale launched into a long and involved speech in French which Leo and I hardly understood a word of. We did, however, pick up words like "Zagora" so we knew Teasdale was telling our whole adventure.

The Frenchman's wide hazel eyes almost fell out of his head by the time Teasdale had finished.

"Mon Dieu!" he gasped, reaching for his wine. *"C'est horrible!"*

After he had drained his glass he offered us a late breakfast. We were so famished we decided to eat there before heading home, for among other things we learned we'd had the good fortune to end up on top of a bus bound for Marrakech. So we were back home, or almost.

As we munched merrily on croissants and sipped café au lait out of large round bowls, Teasdale and our host chatted nonstop in French. It turned out the Frenchman, Gérard Bonnefoys, who'd ordered all the rugs as gifts for his family back in France, knew all about French poetry. So the two had a lot to talk about. In fact, they became fast friends and still correspond with each other.

"Christopher Columbus!" exclaimed Beth as we found our way to Ed Greyley's door around forty minutes later. "Won't they be surprised to see us!"

Chapter XIX

An Afternoon in the Atlas Café

As we later learned, Granny Bea had not been idle during our absence. The moment she learned of our disappearance she sprung into action.

"It was evident I had best do something on the double," she told us afterward. "Fearing you three might end up being kidnapped yourselves, I was determined to bring the mastermind out into the open!"

So, taking pen in hand, Granny Bea sent identical unsigned letters to Jalil, Ed Greyley and Lord Hodgson. The letters read:

"All is known! Come to the Atlas Café to be told what we want! Come or we contact the authorities! Be there at 11:30.
                    Signed,
                        Someone Who Knows All!"

"You see," explained our granny, "I felt sure the mastermind would come. And if the others came merely out of curiosity, so much the better. We'd know exactly who was who!"

Except for a group of three old men sipping peppermint

tea, the café was empty when our granny arrived. She ordered tea to calm her nerves and waited.

Within five minutes, Jalil, who'd entered and had been looking around anxiously, caught sight of Granny Bea and started smiling happily.

"What in heaven's name can he be smiling about?" Granny Bea had wondered.

"So," said Jalil as he quickly walked over to our granny's table and sat down, "don't tell me you got one of those letters, too!"

"Don't play innocent with me, Jalil Khaldouni!" Granny Bea replied in a low voice. "I know all there is to know about you!"

The color drained from Jalil's face and he began twiddling his thumbs nervously. "Who told you?" he asked in a quiet voice.

"No one told me," boasted Granny Bea. "I find things out for myself!"

"Does Ed Greyley know?" asked Jalil suddenly. "He'd fire me for sure if he knew!"

"I doubt you would be able to continue working for him anyway when you are imprisoned on kidnapping charges!" said Granny Bea severely.

"Kidnapping charges!" gasped Jalil. "What are you talking about?"

"Are you or are you not the mastermind?" demanded Granny Bea point-blank.

"You think I'm involved with those kidnappings?" cried Jalil. "Are you crazy?"

"Not in the slightest!" sniffed Granny Bea. "And if you are as innocent as you claim why did you show up when you received the letter?"

"Can you keep a secret?" asked Jalil, and after Granny Bea had proclaimed herself trustworthy as the Bank of England Jalil continued, "Nobody knows it but there *is* a reason why I'm always hanging around Ed Greyley's house: Habiba is my mother!"

"Even in Morocco," snorted our granny, "it surely is not against the law to have a mother! I demand to know what you've been doing snooping around Mr. Greyley's establishment!"

"Well," began Jalil, "I think there's something funny going on with his computer company, and I've been doing some investigating on the sly. A lot of things I've discovered just don't add up!"

"Such as?"

"Such as he seems to have done something to his home computer so it automatically multiplies by ten any deposits made to the list of company earnings! And it divides by ten any withdrawal!"

"Merciful heavens!" exclaimed our granny. "What more perfect way to embezzle!"

"Right!" agreed Jalil. "Greyley *is* up to something! In fact, I've even been paying different people around town to learn things about Ed."

"So," Granny Bea said, half to herself and half to Jalil, "Ed Greyley is not the mastermind, just a common embezzler. . . . Covering up his racing debts, no doubt."

"He could be both mastermind *and* embezzler," suggested Jalil.

"Possibly," admitted Granny Bea. "But I demand to know why *you* did not just quit Mr. Greyley's company if you suspected him of wrong doing?"

"Do you have any idea how hard it is to find work nowadays in Morocco? Unemployment is sky-high! And besides, I'm proud to be a Moroccan and I'm tired of foreigners coming in and robbing us! So I've stayed on with the hope of exposing Ed Greyley."

"Hmmm," Granny Bea replied. "Do you think Lord Hodgson is in on it with Mr. Greyley?"

"I tend to doubt it," considered Jalil. "He seems an honest sort to me."

"Well," sniffed Granny Bea, "if Lord Hodgson is as honest as you say, what is he doing here in this café?"

For there, at the door, elegant as always but nervous as a cat, stood Lord Hodgson.

"I don't believe it!" exclaimed Jalil. "But it's got to be him! We can't let him get away!" he added in a low voice.

Lord Hodgson, however, seemed to have no intention of "getting away." Upon seeing Granny Bea and Jalil he broke into a broad grin and also joined them at their table.

"What a relief!" he began in his clear voice. "I was quite convinced I was the sole victim of some lunatic sending out bizarre anonymous letters!"

Fixing Lord Hodgson with an icy stare, Granny Bea said: "Tell it to the Marines! We happen to know all there is to know about you, and more besides!"

"Right!" added Jalil. "So if I were you I'd just confess and get it over with!"

Suddenly Lord Hodgson lost all the color in his face and his mouth started twitching. "H-how'd you f-find out?" he asked.

"It was far from difficult. My grandchildren observed you at the snake charmer's basket and at this very café, and . . ." she paused for a moment, "my grandson saw you meet with Mister Moustacha!"

"Mister who?" Lord Hodgson asked.

"I mean Mister Moustafa," said Granny Bea quickly.

Lord Hodgson looked down at the dirty table for a few seconds. "I guess I knew all along I'd be found out," he said slowly and sadly. "I guess it's all over now. I'll have to leave Morocco and all I've begun here!"

"If they let you leave, which I for one sincerely doubt," stated Granny Bea. "I should imagine a long stay in prison would be the punishment for a kidnapping crook!"

"A what?" demanded Lord Hodgson.

"She said a kidnapping crook," said Jalil.

"Kidnapping!" exclaimed Lord Hodgson. "What sort of animal do you take me for? Kidnapping is the lowest form of crime imaginable! Only a depraved and disgusting creature would stoop to such a detestable act!"

"Precisely," stated Granny Bea. "So why did you do it?"

"I did no such thing!" said Lord Hodgson primly.

"Then why are you here?" asked Jalil.

"It seems to me I could ask you the same question," Lord Hodgson replied in an annoyed voice. "However," he continued, "I might as well tell you. It had to come out sooner or later, and living under this continual strain is simply destroying my marriage. . . . But promise you'll keep it a secret until I have time to tell Lady Hodgson."

"Of course," agreed our granny and Jalil, feeling very confused.

"When I was a very young man," commenced Lord Hodgson, "only eighteen, I believe, I visited Morocco. At that time it was still a colony. I was, I regret to say, a foolish and impetuous youngster, and unfortunately ran afoul of the law over a small matter I do not care to discuss. As things turned out, I was expelled from the country and returned in disgrace to England—though keeping the reason for my abrupt departure a secret from even my closest friends. Decades went by and Lady Hodgson and myself, who found ourselves for a variety of reasons in economic hardship, came to Morocco, where she had connections which allowed us to begin a small business. At the time I felt quite confident that my previous record would have been lost or forgotten when Morocco achieved independence. At first it seemed as though I was correct. I had no difficulty entering the country and all seemed well. Then, alas, I was recognized on the street by someone who had known me at the time of my early difficulty. As a result I ended up being black-mailed by three people—the snake charmer, Police Chief Moustafa and a younger man to whom I pay money in this café. I paid them to keep my criminal report a secret, for if it came to light, I have little doubt I would be again deported, or perhaps jailed. This sad story I believe explains why I responded to that letter and came here today. I trust you all believe me!"

"Merciful heavens!" exclaimed Granny Bea. "I do! But this means that you aren't the mastermind behind the kid-nappings, and neither is Jalil, so that means . . . that means . . ."

"That means what?" asked Lord Hodgson.

Our granny paused before saying, "That means it has to be Ed Greyley!"

"Someone call my name?" asked a voice and our granny, Jalil and Lord Hodgson wheeled around to see Ed Greyley taking a seat at the table.

"Loathsome kidnapper!" said our granny in an icy voice.

"Now hold your horses, little lady," smiled Ed Greyley. "What are you talking about?"

"Now if that isn't the most ridiculous thing I've ever heard," said Ed Greyley after it all had been explained to him. "For one thing, if I were the kidnapper, why would I go kidnap my own darlin' niece? And for another, you might recall these kidnappings began before I even arrived in Mar-rakech! Isn't that so?"

"You're right there," admitted Jalil. "I don't know why I didn't think of that before. The kidnappings began six months ago and Ed's only been in Marrakech four! But about that monkey-business with the computer . . ."

145

Ed Greyley, looking quite embarrassed, said slowly, "Well—I must admit I have had a few gambling debts and maybe I was fiddlin' around with that old computer to see if I could locate some extra cash. . . . But I surely never embezzled and I surely never kidnapped anybody!"

"My, my," sighed our granny. "Perhaps we *were* barking up the wrong tree!"

"It sure 'nuff appears that way," said Ed with great relief. "But tell me, little lady, what made you so doggone sure it was me, Jalil, or Lord Hodgson? I do declare that this ol' town is just teemin' with suspects—people like the snake charmer and the Police Chief and who knows else!"

"I am afraid you have a point there," our granny replied. "I imagine we just got carried away. I shall have to have a stern word with my grandchildren upon their return! But oh dear! I thought this meeting would help us find them!"

"Now, don't you fret," Ed consoled our granny. "Remember, no ransom note has been received for your young 'uns. No doubt they're just off a-havin' fun. They sure are a rambunctious bunch of buckaroos! Now, I must mosey on home. I hate to leave my darlin' niece alone after all she's been through!"

"Then we shall accompany you," our granny announced wearily as the four left the café and headed for Ed Greyley's.

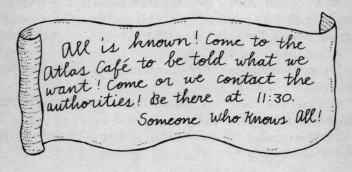

All is known! Come to the Atlas Café to be told what we want! Come or we contact the authorities! Be there at 11:30.
Someone Who Knows All!

Chapter XX

Daniel Turns Detective

"We're home!" we cried as we entered Ed Greyley's.

Habiba, who'd been in the kitchen, ran out to greet us, her arms open wide and tears in her eyes.

Pamela-Ann, the only other person home at the time, eyed us with displeasure.

"Oh," she said, "it's you." A look of interest flickered across her face as she asked, "Were you kidnapped?"

"Sort of," replied Beth. "But only for a while, then we escaped. And, do you know, Pamela-Ann, that we risked our necks to rescue you and instead ended up rescuing Manheim here—"

"*Guten Tag,*" said Manheim primly, bowing in Pamela-Ann's direction.

"Anyway," continued Beth, "we got all the way to Zagora to rescue you, only to find it was all a big mistake—you hadn't even been kidnapped!"

Pamela-Ann's plump chin dropped a few inches and her eyes bugged out in surprise.

"I was so kidnapped!" she said. "And I didn't like it one bit!"

As Manheim called his father on the telephone, Pamela-Ann told us her story.

"The day you all went to the gardens and didn't invite me—" she began.

"We did so!" interrupted Leo.

"Anyway," continued Pamela-Ann, "I thought I'd go for a picnic all by myself so my uncle made me a sandwich and gave me some cookies and off I went. I thought I'd go to the Aguedal Gardens too, but when I got there I was so hungry I ate lunch right away. Then I felt all yucky and hot and tired and I fell asleep. When I woke up I was in a dark room and all tied up and I didn't like it one bit! So I guessed I'd been kidnapped. Later, someone came in and made me eat some dinner and I fell asleep again. When I woke up, there I was back in the gardens. So I took a taxi home and I learned my uncle had paid forty thousand dollars worth of Moroccan money to get me back!" Here she turned to Teasdale and added, "Your father only paid twenty thousand for you, so that means I'm worth more! So there!"

"Christopher Columbus!" exclaimed Beth. "They must have drugged you! Did you happen to get a glimpse of the guy who brought you dinner?"

"No—the room was dark, and I was blindfolded," replied Pamela-Ann. "But I did do something real smart!"

"Namely?"

"When I had one hand untied so I could feed myself, I secretly stashed my bracelet between the mattress I was on and the wall. And I also put the peel from the banana I was eating there, so if the police ever find the room, my bracelet and the banana peel will be there as important evidence!"

"So you *were* kidnapped!" cried Beth. "They must have grabbed Manheim by mistake!"

"There was no mistake," stated Manheim, back from speaking with his father. "My father has informed me he received a ransom note demanding twenty thousand dollars for my safe return, which he threw in the trash. In Germany we do not pay ransom demands."

Beth sat down to think.

"This can only mean one thing," she said slowly. "We know there are only three kidnappers and one mastermind, right? Well, all three kidnappers were involved with Manheim, so how could they also kidnap Pamela-Ann?"

"Yes, how?" Manheim wanted to know.

"Easy! There are two different groups of kidnappers! And the ones who nabbed Manheim are the ones who've been doing the kidnappings all along, while the ones who stole Pamela-Ann are a new bunch!" explained Beth.

"And you have caught neither!" reprimanded Manheim.

"At least we rescued you!" countered Beth as the front door opened and in walked our granny, Ed Greyley, Jalil and Lord Hodgson, fresh from their session at the Atlas Café. Our dad was with them, having run into them on the street.

"Beth! Teasdale! Leo!" cried our granny, flying across the courtyard to give us hugs that squeezed all the air from our lungs.

Of course our dad also hugged us silly.

Ed asked Habiba to make sandwiches and tea while we introduced Manheim to everyone, and then we all sat down to compare stories.

When our dad heard about our dance début, he laughed and said that he'd read in that morning's paper about a riot by Japanese tourists in a hotel in Zagora, and had wondered if we'd somehow been involved!

Our granny, however, was in a more somber state of mind.

"Just think!" she snorted. "We are now confronted with two groups of kidnappers! What a shocking state of affairs!"

But Ed Greyley scoffed at the notion of two groups of kidnappers. "I don't buy that idea," he told us. "I say they have just expanded their operations."

"Nonsense!" sniffed our granny. "Their ways of operating when they kidnapped Teasdale and Manheim appear quite different from when they kidnapped Pamela-Ann. For one, they asked for a different amount of money, for another they accepted payment in Moroccan currency, and for another, they did not compel Pamela-Ann to write you a note. We're dealing with *two* kidnapping rings! I say this country is unsafe for both man and beast!"

And speaking of beasts, it was at this moment Ed Greyley got his first view of Daniel. Up to that time, Daniel had been residing out of sight in Teasdale's shirt, but the smell of the snack Habiba was preparing caused him to poke his head out and look around hopefully.

"What is that?" demanded Ed.

"Daniel the Monkey Smith," explained Teasdale.

Ed was not impressed.

"Monkey's do not belong at tables!" he told us. "I don't want my darlin' niece a-gettin' fleas on her food!"

"But if you please," pleaded Teasdale, "Daniel has no fleas! Nor has he lice. He's both clean and nice!"

But Ed insisted Daniel be locked up in Leo and Teasdale's room during the meal, so we had to imprison him upstairs. But it made us laugh to see, while Habiba was in the midst of bringing the food out from the kitchen, Daniel scramble out of the little window above Leo and Teasdale's door. From there he leapt onto a hanging lamp on the balcony. He swung back and forth from the lamp a few times, and then jumped to the door next to Leo and Teasdale's, and climbed through the small window above it.

Habiba was just serving Ed a large sandwich when something odd caught Beth's eye. It was Daniel. He was perched on the railing of the balcony, busily playing with two objects.

"Christopher Columbus!" cried Beth, giving Leo a swift kick. Without speaking, Beth instructed Leo to look up at Daniel. Leo's mouth fell open with shock. He then looked quizzically at Beth. Beth looked back, then said, "Excuse me, but may I be excused?"

"Certainly," our granny replied, and seconds later Beth was up on the balcony with Daniel. He handed her the objects he'd been playing with and bounded off to find amusement elsewhere.

Back at the table, Beth handed the objects to Leo under the table.

"What are you young 'uns handin' back and forth?" Ed Greyley wanted to know.

"I don't think you want to know," Beth replied.

"If you brought that monkey back to the table, I'm a-gonna tan your hides!" announced Ed as he stood up and stalked over to our side of the table. And before we knew what had happened, Ed had reached down and grabbed what Beth had been holding—a bracelet and a banana peel!

"Where'd you—" began Ed when Pamela-Ann interrupted in an excited voice.

"That's my bracelet! And that's the banana peel I hid! How'd you get them?"

"They were in the storage room next to Leo and Teasdale's room!" burst out Beth.

"But only my uncle has the key to that room!" said Pamela-Ann, looking momentarily confused. Then, as she made sense of what she'd seen, she just stared at her uncle with her mouth open.

Then, as we watched in horror, Ed threw the bracelet and banana peel across the courtyard and with one hand grabbed Teasdale, and with the other a knife.

Holding the knife to Teasdale's throat, Ed began backing away, dragging Teasdale toward the door.

"Nobody move and the boy'll be all right," he said.

We sat speechless, but Pamela-Ann leapt to her feet and started shrieking.

"You're a yucky uncle!" she cried. "Why'd you kidnap me? Your own niece! That's not fair!"

"I never meant to hurt you, Pamela-Ann," replied Ed as he inched toward the door, still clutching Teasdale, who by this time was as white as vanilla ice cream

"Then why?" howled Pamela-Ann.

Ed gave a mighty yawn then answered: "'Cause I just happen to have a little ol' gamblin' problem and I lost a little too much at the track, so I ended up borrowin' close to forty thousand dollars from the company to pay off my debts. Then I tried to cover it up by fiddlin' around with the computer. But I knew that would never fool Nicholas Andrews or anyone who examined the records too closely. Then I had the idea of blackmailin' Lord Hodgson. I knew there was something fishy in his past and I started bribin' people to tell me all about him. But then I realized he didn't have enough to pay me the money I needed. . . . So I figured with all these kidnappings goin' on I'd just go and fake one. That way I could pretend to pay the ransom out of company money. That would explain all the missin' money. I'd say it was what I had to pay for Pamela-Ann's release."

"But wouldn't you just have to pay it back later?" wondered Manheim, still asking the hard questions.

"Not if I skipped the country," yawned Ed, "the way I'm a-doin' now. You call the airport and book me a seat out of here, and one for Teasdale too. I'll let him go unharmed when I'm safely out of Morocco!"

Teasdale made a face and said:

"Your invitation is generous and fine,
But I'd rather stay with this family of—"

"Oh, shut up!" barked Ed. "You give me a pain!" he added, dragging Teasdale a step closer to the door.

"I forbid you to take my grandson!" announced our granny, rising to her feet. "Take me instead!"

"I'll do as I please, little lady," Ed answered with a yawn. "Remember, I'm the one with the knife!"

"You're a monster!" Granny Bea stated.

Our granny wasn't the only angry one, Teasdale also had had enough.

"Being kidnapped once was not very nice," he told Ed Greyley, "so I refuse to be kidnapped twice!"

"Teasdale!" cried Beth. "Don't do anything dumb! He's got a knife!"

But Teasdale started wriggling to get free. Ed looked furious and raised his knife as if to strike.

"Ed, don't!" cried our dad.

But with a wide sweeping motion, Ed lunged the knife toward Teasdale's chest. But just as it seemed the blade would surely pierce Teasdale's skin, Ed paused, gave an enormous yawn, looked around with a dazed expression . . . and fell suddenly to the ground, fast asleep!

"What the—" said a shocked Beth as we all dashed to comfort Teasdale.

Teasdale was trembling, Ed was snoring, and we were all confused.

"What a peculiar time to take a nap!" commented Granny Bea, hugging Teasdale. We all watched as our dad and Jalil tied up Ed in case he woke up. Manheim meanwhile was comforting Pamela-Ann, who was still shaking with rage over what we'd just discovered.

"Do not worry," Manheim was saying, "where I come from uncles are well-behaved!"

Habiba then appeared with tea to calm our nerves. She also said something in rapid Arabic to Jalil that made him start laughing.

"This will explain why Ed fell asleep," Jalil told us. "The

sandwich Habiba gave Ed to eat was filled with the same drugged meat Ed had given Pamela-Ann when he kidnapped her! It seems that earlier, the day Pamela-Ann was 'kidnapped,' Habiba saw Ed throw some meat in the trash. Unhappy about wasting food, she fed some of it to her pet cat, who promptly fell asleep. So Habiba, who had never liked Ed Greyley very much anyway, kept the remaining meat and today gave it to Ed to see what would happen!"

"*Chokeran!*" cried Teasdale, which means "thank you" in Arabic, and ran to give Habiba a big hug.

Teasdale then chuckled and commented:

> "It's the funniest joke under the sun,
> The hunter was captured by his own gun!"

"Yet," pointed out our granny, "we should be remiss in celebrating too heartily. The other kidnappers are, after all, still at large, and we have not a clue as to their identity."

"You may not, but I do," said Manheim proudly.

"What?"

"When I was first kidnapped, here in Marrakech, I was held in a dirty apartment while the kidnappers were deciding where to take me."

"So?"

"So, during this time they put in a few phone calls to the person you call the mastermind. And I know the number they dialed!"

"But how?" we asked.

"By listening, of course," Manheim replied primly. "I listened as the dial went around to see how long it took. Thus I know the number of the mastermind!"

"Oh, Manheim," cooed Pamela-Ann, "I knew you could do it!"

"Of course I could," said Manheim with a smile.

154

"So what's the number?" demanded Beth.

Manheim concentrated before saying, "942-61-21."

All color drained from Jalil's face as he stared open-mouthed at Lord Hodgson. Lord Hodgson also had his mouth open wide.

"The number you just told," explained Jalil, "happens to be Lord Hodgson's!"

"B-but I didn't have anything to do with it!" protested Lord Hodgson.

"You know," interrupted our granny, "I believe you."

"So do I," agreed Jalil.

"But that means—that means," began Lord Hodgson. "That means—"

"That means nobody moves!" said an icy voice from the doorway.

155

Chapter XXI

The Hand Behind the Gun

There stood Lady Hodgson, and she was holding a gun.

"Cynthia—" started Lord Hodgson in a stunned voice. "Whatever—"

"Shut up and put your hands in the air!" commanded Lady Hodgson. "All of you! And fast!"

Up went all our hands (except Ed Greyley's, since he was still unconscious and tied up on the floor).

"I don't understand—" began Lord Hodgson.

"I'm sure you don't," Lady Hodgson replied simply. "But how on earth do you think I managed to buy such expensive clothing and exquisite jewelry on your paltry earnings? And don't think I don't know how much goes to paying off blackmailers either! No, for quite some time I have been masterminding the kidnappings here in Marrakech!"

"But—"

"Hush!" snapped Lady Hodgson. "I shall have to put in an emergency call to Achmed, Fatah, and Saïd and let them dispose of you in whatever manner they see fit!"

"Dispose of us?" gasped our granny. "Surely you do not mean—"

"That's precisely what I mean," Lady Hodgson replied. "I cannot afford to let you go free knowing what you now know! I have no desire to spend the remainder of my days in a Moroccan jail!"

"But that would be murder!" our dad said.

"So be it!" Lady Hodgson remarked.

"But I'm your husband!" Lord Hodgson cried.

"You have been an inconvenience to me far too long, Lionel," was Lady Hodgson's terse reply.

Poor Lord Hodgson was trembling with shock, Pamela-Ann was whimpering and Teasdale was gazing upward toward the balcony above Lady Hodgson's well-coiffed head. Beth imagined he must be praying.

"Now," said Lady Hodgson, "I shall lock you in one of the rooms until my men show up. I suggest if you want to say your prayers, now would be a good time to do so."

Leave it to Teasdale to step forward. He cleared his throat and said:

> "I pray to you up on high,
> Let it fall now, that's my cry!
> Drop it now, not later on,
> Or we'll all be dead and gone!"

"What a peculiar prayer," commented Lady Hodgson, just as there was a flash of silver, an odd bang, and a quick high shriek, followed by a heavy thud as Lady Hodgson fell unconscious to the courtyard floor.

"Maybe she had some of Ed's sandwich?" suggested Beth after she'd grabbed Lady Hodgson's gun off the tiled floor.

Teasdale once again cleared his throat and spoke:

> "No, it wasn't a sandwich at all,
> But Daniel the Monkey who answered my call!
> Look up above and you will see
> The one who saved both you and me!"

We all looked up, and there dangling from the balcony overhead and chattering loudly, swung Daniel. Teasdale had spotted him, playing with the shiny silver tea server he found so attractive, and immediately composed a poetic prayer commanding him to drop it right on Lady Hodgson's head.

"She always hated those silver tea servers," said a stunned Lord Hodgson, "but I don't imagine she really had a good reason until now!"

Chapter XXII

One Final Surprise

The Air Maroc jet was cruising smoothly toward New York as we sat merrily eating and drinking in our luxurious first-class seats. Normally we travel coach, but to thank us for capturing the kidnappers and Ed Greyley, the Moroccan government had sent us home first-class.

"This champagne is not altogether odious," declared our granny, who still hadn't got over the shock of being so wrong about Jalil.

After Daniel had knocked out Lady Hodgson with the flying teapot, things had happened quickly. Jalil called the police and to everyone's surprise Police Chief Moustacha arrived immediately and carted Lady Hodgson and Ed Greyley off to jail—and without losing either of them! He also commanded some of his officers to round up Achmed, Fatah and Saïd. By the way, this turned out to be Moustacha's last official act as Police Chief of Marrakech; the next day he was assigned to be Police Chief in a small village in the western part of the country.

Needless to say, the two people most shocked by our solving of the crimes were Pamela-Ann and Lord Hodgson. Pamela-Ann said that having a crook for an uncle was the yuckiest thing she'd ever heard of. Since her parents were still unreachable, for a dreadful moment we were scared we'd have to take Pamela-Ann home with us. But Manheim came to the rescue: He'd apparently taken a shine to Pam, so he invited her to spend a few weeks with him and his family. Pamela-Ann, who'd also taken quite a shine to Manheim, agreed readily. Beth thinks those two deserve each other!

Poor Lord Hodgson went into a deep depression after finding out that his wife was the mastermind. He even wanted to go back to England and try to start a new life. But Granny Bea sternly told him he'd be a fool to do that; he should instead stay in Marrakech and see if he could salvage the computer company despite all the money Ed Greyley had gambled away. He ended up taking Granny Bea's advice and decided to make Jalil an equal partner. Nicholas Andrews turned out to be a very understanding sort of fellow, and gave Lord Hodgson and Jalil a long time to repay his loan. Finally, the Moroccan government pardoned Lord Hodgson for whatever it was he had done so long ago.

As for Jalil, he moved into Ed Greyley's house with Habiba. We learned too that the reason Jalil was able to dress so well on his meagre income was that Habiba gave him some of the money Ed Greyley paid her so he could look more elegant and further his career.

Before we left we'd learned Lady Hodgson, Ed Greyley, and Lady Hodgson's henchmen were given incredibly long prison terms for their crimes. And our dad told us that Moroccan prisons were especially severe, something Granny Bea heartily approved of. "Really!" she exclaimed, "it is beyond my comprehension why criminals think they should be treated like guests when they have committed some foul crime! I hope Lady Hodgson is compelled to live on bread and water!"

Teasdale, however, was feeling a little blue because our dad said he couldn't bring Daniel home with us. "I doubt they even allow monkeys on airplanes," our dad told us. Although Jalil promised to adopt Daniel and take good care of him, it had been a tearful parting anyway. Teasdale even claimed Daniel cried! Of course Teasdale made up a farewell poem about Daniel, part of which went:

"Now I say good-bye to Daniel,
A better pet than Golden Retriever or Spaniel!
I must go and he must stay,
And I'll miss him each and ev'ry day!"

The entire poem went on for twelve pages and I have to say that Daniel listened attentively the whole time Teasdale was reading to him, so maybe he liked it. Beth has to admit that it wasn't one of the best poems Teasdale had ever written. But don't tell Teasdale I said so! Teasdale says having a poem written about you is a great honor.

And on the subject of honors, before we left Morocco, the Mayor of Marrakech invited us to his house for a special feast. We were presented with the keys of the city, certificates of merit from the Moroccan government and free tickets to return the next year on Air Maroc. We even received a reward for capturing the kidnappers which we had to share with Manheim because it was he who had remembered the phone number. But our dad made us give our share to Lord Hodgson to help him pay off the money Ed Greyley had embezzled. Our dad also got back the twenty thousand dollars he'd ransomed Teasdale with. Anyway, it was a great feast and they even had Moroccan dancers—though luckily not our friend from Zagora! We also got to invite all the friends we'd made, people like Habiba, Jalil and Lord Hodgson, of course, but also Gérard Bonnefoys and Arielle Dor-léac. Our dad made us invite Pamela-Ann and Manheim. We even asked Kensaku Yamatori! He wasn't quite sure why he'd been invited and spent the entire evening telling us about a beautiful Moroccan dancer he'd met in Zagora!

"Yes," mused our granny, gazing out the airplane window, "We certainly have had our share of adventures!"

"May I fill up your glass of champagne?" asked the stewardess. She then turned to our dad and asked, "Would you like an extra bottle of milk for the baby?"

"Baby?" wondered our dad. "What baby?"

"Oh, you're such a tease!" smiled the stewardess. "I mean the baby your son is holding."

"Christopher Columbus!" laughed Beth. For there, in his seat on the other side of the aisle, sat Teasdale, happily giving a bottle to a little baby named Daniel!

Jalil Teasdale Leo Beth Pomela Kensaku Y. Manheim

HABIBA Ann

Mrs. B. Smith L. Hodgson

photo by our Dad